Not the Home I Dreamed About

Josine Mutuyimana

ISBN: 978-1-952263-04-0

Dedication

I want to dedicate this book to my mom, Jeanne, and my sister, Ange, with whom I shared every memory in this book.

Acknowledgment

I want to thank all the beautiful souls that made this book possible. Without you, I wouldn't have the strength to make this happen!

Thank You.

About the Author

Josine Mutuyimana was born in the wilderness of the Democratic Republic of Congo. Her childhood was difficult and plagued with extreme conditions. Josine always saw education as a resource that would help her family escape from their circumstances. Her roots originally laid in Rwanda, from where the family had migrated to Congo due to the civil war and political conflicts.

She worked hard to achieve excellent results in esteemed schools until she was given a fully-funded scholarship for her college education in the USA. One by one, all of her dreams came true, from education to providing for her family, and of finding a place, she would call her home.

Throughout her childhood, Josine fantasized about finding her way back to home and dreamt of the beauty and love she would feel there. In this book, she relays her journey and wishes to inspire the readers with her story giving a message of hope, fortitude, and hard work.

Preface

My mom used to tell me to try and fail but never fail to try, and this has been my life motto ever since I was a little child. Trying, I continue to believe, is a sign that you are doing something; failing, on the other hand, is a sign that you are at least trying.

I was born in a refugee camp in the Democratic Republic of Congo, where everything felt foreign since the day I learned that this place was not home. We had moved to Congo because of a great political turmoil rumbling in Rwanda, which was my home. That was why my childhood passed in the neighboring country.

Coming through what my family and I came through, you would think we were low on hope. In spite of all that came, the only torch that built inside me was of hope, the hope for a home. I had never seen Rwanda in real life, but I had dreamt of it in my imagination every single day. It was my greatest fantasy as a child. I knew that there is a place that is beautiful, peaceful, and sparkling that I could call home out there. But it was just out of my reach. I used to spend my entire time making scenarios in my head of what Rwanda is like. A typical fantasy-prone child, you know. I would ask my mom questions about Rwanda and about our relatives that lived there. Out of what mom would tell me, I would imagine my relatives, living close to each other; I would envision myself going house to house, springing upon them and wrapping them in hugs; I would imagine eating delicacies in their homes; I would imagine myself sleeping in the same bed with my cousins, surrounded by love and smiling faces; I would also imagine myself going to school and making friends for the first time.

In the refugee camp where we lived, some of this was possible, but there was a missing sentiment to it. Something was lacking from it. It was like eating noodles with a spoon, you can eat it, but it just doesn't feel right. We resided alone in the forest with no opportunity to make any friends, no real delicacies to eat, and no cousins.

That being said, there was always this aching desire for home. When I was nearly five years old, I was a content kid. My life consisted of living with both parents, with uncles who visited, and there was no room to imagine a different life. I failed to understand why we lived where I was born. I simply accepted it, thinking that our life has been that way and will always be that way. I was a child; after all, you don't truly start questioning these things that early.

Though that wasn't the case as I grew up. I felt more, and I wanted so much more...

Contents

Page Left Blank Intentionally

My Roots

My daddy was a beverage distributor. He used to come back home carrying avocados after work. I loved them so much. There was another thing I was very fond of, and that was watching my father's throat work as he would drink. As soon as he would arrive home, I would hand him water and watch him drink it. He used to chug it down quickly, making little gurgling sounds in his throat. As silly as it sounds, I would watch him do it all day long.

. Daddy was a very kind and loving man, tall and incredibly handsome. When he returned from work, he would lift me and poke my belly, asking me how my day went. Evenings were the only time I could see him. He used to wake up very early in the morning, much before my elder sister, Ange, and I would get up and leave for work. Over the weekends, daddy used to take us sisters for a walk and show us around.

He once took us to the market and bought skirts and shirts for us. I mean, he took us out a lot of times, but this was one of those days before things went terrible. The mind embellishes the memories of times before adversity struck, I guess. We had an Uncle named Alex, who was the tallest man I had ever seen in my young days. He was 24 years old, skinny, and used to live in the same camp as us. His stories were very entertaining, especially because he used to add elements of fiction into real stories. We had a phrase for this in my local language, and we called adding things to stories that never happened as 'having a sweet tongue.' Uncle Alex never bought us gifts, but I loved his stories. He would also carry us on his back and play with us, fueling out imagination with his stories. I loved him so much.

My other favorite uncle was my mom's brother named Gisa. He was 26 years old and lived with us. He seemed to be jobless since he was always around, unlike my daddy. He was loving and a cheerful character, always equipped with a wide smile and immense love for children. He would gather all the kids in the camp and play with them. I loved him, as well.

Gisa and Alex were best friends, and they used to hang out almost every day. They were kind of like the Harold and Kumar of our family. Wherever Alex was, you would conveniently find Gisa there as well. They sometimes used to talk about girls in the camp, and they never allowed us to get close to them when having such conversations. They used to go around together, exploring our neighborhood. It was a new country for them, like for the other refugees in the camp. One day Gisa and Alex walked a little farther than they used to go, and they were met with gunfire. One bullet bit off Gisa's finger, and he nearly got killed. The two friends came back running, intact, except one of my uncles missing a finger. Alex immediately began narrating the situation to my daddy, telling him how men armed with guns ran after them and how Gisa lost his finger, and they buried it immediately.

You would think things would have gotten tense, quite the opposite. I mean, it was Uncle Alex after all. He made the story more dramatic and funny, especially the part where Gisa lost his finger. He could describe how scared Gisa looked, eyes wide open, and how he jumped to pick his finger up after the bullet cut it. We all laughed so hard but also felt sorry for Gisa.

And that was when I first realized how much danger we were in and how unsafe our camp was. And the camp only grew more unsafe since then. People were reported missing and were getting killed every day. No person should be in a situation similar to that. My dad decided that we should shift somewhere safer.

The Democratic Republic Of Congo is a vast country, and switching camps consisted of just walking until we got tired. That was the beginning of our nomadic life. We eventually moved to a closed neighborhood, a hundred miles away from our previous location, and stayed there for a year. My sister joined an elementary school in the neighborhood, and my daddy continued his beverage distribution business.

I would sometimes follow my sister to school and sit with her in the class. Not that I was enthusiastic about learning, I just wanted to cause mischief. I was very stubborn and would spur a disturbance in the class, asking my sister to lend me one of her pencils so that I could write as well. I would also raise my hand whenever the teacher asked a question, and my sister would immediately pull my hand down because I had no idea what they were even studying.

After school, my sister would report everything to my daddy. She wanted him never to allow me to follow her at school again. I loved going to school for my own evil purposes. I mean, what even is a childhood that is empty of fun and mischief. My sister refused to go with me the next morning, saying her teacher has told her that I distract everyone in the class. I wasn't supposed to be there, to begin with, because I was too young for the class. We lived next to other Congolese families and among them lived a young man, somewhere in his 20s. He seemed to be our family friend as used to pass by our house almost every day. He owned a sugarcane farm, and he would bring us some sugarcanes time and again. One day he asked my mom if he could take me to the sugarcane farm.

I was thrilled because I loved the sugar cane, and so my mother allowed. The farm was very close to our house, and he took me there. I liked him at that moment when he gave me a bunch of sugar cane. I enjoyed them with a wholesome pleasure. But the man's evil intent eventually showed, and it haunted me later.

Since that day, this excursion became a routine, and one that would scar me for life. He would pick me up at the same time every day, and take me to the sugarcane plantation. I would get one small sugar cane, and he would wait until I finished it so that we could go home. The second time was when the sexual abuse began. While I would be eating my sugar cane, he would sit me down on his lap, remove my underwear, and make his penis touch my vagina. I was, of course, too young to know what was going on, especially because it did not hurt, for there was no penetration. But it still felt wrong. Remember eating noodles with a spoon? Somewhat like that. My mom never noticed anything wrong, either, because I was never physically hurt. This happened almost every day during the four months that we stayed there. I honestly could not register what was going on. Not at that time, at least. Not until for the next 13 years, until it had finally sunk in. I was 18 years old when I found out that I was sexually molested and almost got raped.

That was when I had my first boyfriend. My boyfriend had casually hugged me tightly, and something changed in me right away. It came flooding in my mind, the memory that I had stifled. I recalled what happened to me in that sugarcane plantation. I burst into tears at the flashback, while my boyfriend stood there confused, asking if it was him who did something wrong. I didn't tell him anything.

My world turned darker from that day onwards. I realized and felt sick at the thought of a stranger taking advantage of me when I was only a 5 years old innocent girl. It also struck me how my family never suspected the real intent of the man who was taking me to his sugarcane plantation every day. I started feeling really disgusted at myself and my body for the first time. And really, what can an immature girl do but blame herself after registering all of this trauma? I had no counselor let alone have anyone to talk about it with. My shame kept me from it. I spent nights thinking about it, wondering if anything else had happened - if I was blocking any other memory out. I became filled with angst, filled with rage paired with disgust, but I also knew that there was no one to blame. I tried to force myself to forget it, but that never happened. In the end, I decided to carry it with me and bury it in my heart.

Even today, no one knows that this has happened to me. It is only in this book that my mom will also find out, just like everyone else. These are some of the things that my heart carries and thank God for the blessing that writing is. It feels better to be writing about rather than talking.

It's dazzling how many things that happen when you are a child can affect your adulthood. Even the smallest of things that one cannot remember will have in some way shaped us into our adult life. Political instability in Congo kept getting worse. The Rwandans were being hunted in the country, which meant that my sister stopped attending school, and all of us, save daddy, stayed inside the house.

My daddy would still sneak out and go to work for us to survive. We changed our camps again because my dad had been told that 'they' were coming to kill us and 'they' knew our house. We comforted ourselves with the thought that if we temporarily move to another house, it will save us and buy us some time. After that, we could probably plan to move somewhere far from where we were staying.

My mom had been seven months pregnant then for a baby number four. She was pregnant almost every year since she got married, and was sick nearly every day of keeping up with her pregnancies. They were harsher than regular pregnancies. What worried us was when some of our neighbors said that her pregnancy was poisoned. It was neither supposed to be so painful nor should have been making her sick so frequently.

My pregnant mom could hardly do anything at home. All the responsibilities fell on my sister and me. We had to do all the house chores regardless of us being seven and five years old. My dad was always out until the evenings. It was a strange time to live through. One morning my dad woke up like usual, and I insisted that we go together to his work. I had not been going to any other place other than our house ever since I stopped following my sister to school. Dad must have had some mercy on me. He complied with my pleading. I went with him to work, but before getting there, we saw a group of men who looked like soldiers with no uniforms. They had guns, and they were waiting for my dad right outside the place he worked. They had been informed that he was a Rwandan.

As we caught sight of the soldiers, my dad, sensing danger, instantly pushed me away. He told me to stay there and make no sound. He then went straight to the soldiers so that they don't come near to where I was hidden. You can imagine he was smart enough to know that if they found out we were together, they might kill both of us. He did not hide, instead he served himself up to the soldiers to manipulate all of their attention on him.

I watched as they dragged my dad on the ground and took him with them. I, a girl of 5, did not know what was going on, but I knew they were terrible people who were harming daddy. I stayed there for two hours, waiting for my father to return to me. What else could I have done? My father instructed me to stay still so that I couldn't follow him. He had to take me home.

In my heart, I knew dad would eventually come, and we will go home together. Or, I don't know, I was just comforting myself. I never knew those sights of him heading towards the soldiers, slammed down on the ground and taken away by them, would be the last time I would see my father.

After two hours, I stopped hiding in the place where my father left me after I sensed that the soldiers were gone. I was still careful to take soft steps. There was a lady in hiding nearby who happened to know my dad. She did not seem dangerous to me, had allegedly seen all that passed between my father and the soldiers, and wished to take me back home. We landed home and narrated to my family the whole incident about my father and the soldiers.

The news was an unexpected shock to all. Everybody was still hoping and praying for my dad to come back later in the evening like he always does. The waiting part was nail-biting and kept growing more intense as time passed. Our eyes were locked continuously upon the entrance. A day went by without us hearing any news. Then another day passed until eventually, it had been a week since my dad was taken away. On approximately the eighth day, one of the guys who was captured along with my dad returned with news of what had transpired. All our ears were perked up, and we were listening to him fully focused, surrounding him, holding our tongues to riddle him with questions. He explained that the Rwandans were being taken to be enlisted as soldiers as well to fight for Congo and follow their dirty orders. He told us that he and my dad weren't going to become soldiers. They secretly planned to rebel and escape overnight. They had flown away from their traps and left the place.

But the notorious troops heard their footsteps and ran after them in the dark. The chase went for some time, and shouting and cursing were involved. The soldiers ultimately opened fire from behind, and unfortunately, a bullet caught my father, and he fell. The man told us that he died right there. The other man expressed that he survived through some work of fate, but to us, especially to my mom, fate had been terrible.

I did not fully know what death was. I still had the impression that my dad will return, in spite of being shot and killed, as they said he was. The real shock came to my sick, pregnant mom, however. She was jolted to her roots, and such denial took over her that she did not even react with grief. Or with anything, for that matter. She plainly refused to believe the Rwandan man. Meanwhile, it had also been two days since we had eaten anything, and I was starving. I suppose my mother did make peace with the reality in the end, after all, what alternative did she have? She couldn't stay still at one point, struck with disbelief while her children remained starving. My mom called my sister and me, and she began to explain that my dad was killed, and what it means to die and that he will never come back home.

She seemed to be holding herself courageously, despite the moisture in her eye. I still remember looking at her watery eyes, and I remember how it suddenly took over me how stark the situation is. She told us that we have to grow up and stop acting like little kids that we were. She explained that she was sick and is unable to provide food for us.

She also elaborated that our dad was the only breadwinner, so we should stop asking for food as well since my dad will never come back. It meant that we had to fend for ourselves that time onwards. As young as I was then, I could see my life was changing drastically. I knew that this conversation was one of the hardest we had ever had with our mother. I knew that this was a turning point. After all these realizations, I was especially tenacious to preserve every single word she said inside my heart, especially where she said that we have to grow without our daddy, to be like daddy, who will never, ever return home. I didn't exactly know what to do from there. Watching my mother fight her tears was a scary sight. We had had difficult times, yes, but none that had broken my mother in this manner.

On top of that, there was also the fear of our lives. The soldiers were still out hunting Rwandans. Our lives were in danger; we were no longer safe in even our homes. I would watch one of our neighbors eating cold potatoes, and I wanted so badly to ask for some, but I remembered what my mom had once told me. She had instilled in us never to ask strangers for food, nor to eat anywhere else unless she is there with us or permit us to eat.

My sister and I were famished, and we couldn't keep our eyes away from our neighbor, who was eating potatoes. Yes, at that moment, even they seemed like luxuries. He finally caught hold of our eyes and could sense our hunger, so he gave some of his potatoes to us. They brought the color back in me, I was that happy, and more when I tasted the potatoes and they were scrumptious. I made a mental note to myself, which was also like a promise, that I will cook potatoes in precisely the same manner when I become rich enough to afford them. At that stage, this is how things looked: we had officially lost our dad; my mom was getting closer to her pregnancy due date; we had no food in our one-room house; political instability was deteriorating further. Rwandans were being killed in the Goma area that we were staying in. As a result, we were forced to migrate again to some isolated place with no houses or people around. We had a considerable camping plastic bag that we would bend and make a little house out of. It was convenient because it made moving houses portable.

A few months before my father's murder, my mom's sister, named Charly, had come to live with us. She was 23 years old, tall and slender with black hair and perfect white teeth, all aligned. Numerous men in the village wanted to marry her, but my dad never allowed. He thought that she was too young to marry. Moreover, those men were Congolese, whom Charly did not seem to like. But here's the thing. If a family had a beautiful young lady like Charly, men would definitely be on the lookout to wife her. If she wouldn't agree to it, there was a high risk of getting raped or kidnapped.

My dad had been on the search for a decent Rwandan man for her before something could come upon her, but he couldn't find one. After his passing, my uncles and other friends helped us find the right husband for Charly. They finally found a Rwandese family in the village with a young man who eventually fell in love with Charly. They got married a few months later. Charly's husband had a sister named Annet, who was very helpful to my family, and when she heard that my dad passed away, she came to live with and take care of us, since my mom was too sick to.

Annet went with us everywhere. She would go to the forest to pick fruits, yams, and vegetables for us to eat. In a way, she became our breadwinner. Three weeks in at our new place, in the middle of nowhere, surrounded by the cacophony of animals and birds, we were adjusting into life without dad. I still strangely had some hopes that my dad will be back, which made sense in my head because we hadn't seen his dead body, let alone buried him. Being a child, full of imagination and fantasy, you can barely blame me for keeping my hopes up. Despite that, I would sometimes get scared at the thought that I might never see him again; that he is gone forever.

Not a day went by that I didn't miss my dad, and every day the intensity would grow sharper. Even the thought that we were getting used to a life without him would sadden me. I began crying over his death, which so far I had only been uncertain about. In retrospect, I guess my eyes and heart were making up for the tears I had not shed the day I had lost him. I started having deep thoughts and memories of my dad.

I once gathered my siblings so that we would cry together. It seemed like I was just waking up from my dreams to absorb the reality of the situation. Or I don't know. Maybe I was outgrowing my childhood world of fantasies to accept that my dad passed away. Two months later, I awoke one unforgettable night to hear my mum screaming. I presumed she was wounded since there was blood flowing down her legs.

Regardless, I was a complete stranger to the situation. I touched her, asking her where she felt the pain, but she could not stop screaming. My eyes started to water, thinking that my mum was going to die, since it was my first time to see her crying so blatantly with screams, just like a baby. At that very moment, so many questions ran through my head. *"How is life going to go on without her? What will things be like now? Will we siblings go on to live as orphans? Will we die in this forest without knowing our home country?"* On cue, I burst into tears until I saw Annet carrying a baby boy. This was my first exposure to the concept of pregnancy and birthing a baby. I realized how strong my mum was, facing labor alone without any help, and of course, without any medical equipment. We were now four children, two boys, and two girls, along with my mom and Annet. My mom named our newborn, *"Leo."* He resembled my dad.

We stayed in the same place for three more months; through all the trials and tribulations of a new life among us. It had meant one more mouth to feed, and of course, one can imagine this wasn't going to be easy. My sister and I continued going with Annet to search for food for the whole family.

I was only five years old, but I felt like a grown woman already. It is indeed true what they say, that age is just a number. It is by no means synonymous with maturity and a person's development. Sometimes, while searching for food, I met chimpanzees jumping from tree to tree, expertly swinging across vines too, and I would turn back running, with thorns piercing my shoeless feet. I was afraid that they were swinging towards me, coming to snatch me away and keep me with them. As a result, I often went back home, empty-handed. That meant I had to fall asleep on an empty stomach. More than once, we went for three days without food. Daily hunger was no stranger to us. These days were so bad that sometimes I wished to die since I felt more like an animal than a human being. There was a village three miles away from the forest we were living in at the time.

Annet took us there once, and we saw people and kids at our age. That was when some traces of humanity was awakening again in me. It felt so heartwarming to see kids again after four months of being in the forest, deprived of any human interaction and only wild animals' sounds to busy ourselves with. I loved the kids that we met that day, and I wished I could be one of them or be allowed to stay with them.

They were a sort of reminder for what my siblings and I didn't have, growing up as primitives or savages. Living with them was not possible. I was a Rwandan kid, not a Congolese, unlike them, and Rwandese were still being hunted down. So we needed to stay far from everybody else to be safe, and in this case, to ensure their safety as well.

Still, there was no real harm in infrequent visits, we supposed. So, in the following weeks, we made a few more trips to the village. We were now making friends with children and elders alike. One older woman named Mwabo loved us so much that she would cook Ugali for our welcome. Ugali is an exclusive African dish made from Cassava flour and goes with some soup.

She would sometimes make meat soup, which was delicious to my senses. The meat was from animals which I don't even know about, for I had never had tasted that variety of taste. But did I care much about that? Nope. All I wanted was food, and Mwabo could conjure up some of the most delicious dishes. She eventually became like a grandma to us, calling and treating us like her grandchildren. To her, we were young kids.

The best part was that I felt like a young kid with the way she treated me. Over a mere span of five tender years of my age, I had had experiences that made me feel like a grown woman. But Mwabo made me feel like a child to the core. She introduced us to her extended family and gelled so well that it started to feel like family with them. Sometimes she would check up on us and bring us food at our place.

She became a secretive informer, giving us news and precautions for the bad boys who were chasing and killing Rwandans, or if they were approaching near us. From time to time, upon her information, we would migrate temporarily to other places or sleep somewhere else other than our home. Then, of course, when it was safe again, we would eventually return. Needless to say, it was she who informed us when things grew normal too.

Once, we stayed in the same place for almost five months until her information came that we could come back. We called that place *"Iwacu,"* which means home. When my daddy was still working as a beverage distributor in the refugee camp, he had a client who became his good friend. The man's name was John, and he was also from Rwanda, like everybody else in the refugee camp.

He would spend time with us and eventually grew to become a good family friend. He sometimes used to bring small toys for my sister and me. We liked them, and we liked him. And when John heard from someone that my dad had passed away, he started asking people around about us. He asked about our condition and wellbeing, but especially about where we moved to. People guided him, and he eventually found us at our *"Iwacu"* place. My mom needed somebody like him to talk to, which is understandable. I mean that we were all too young, and an adult's mind could only be understood by another mature one's. They talked and seemed to get along pretty well. He consistently started checking upon us. Almost every week, he would come and bring my mom new clothes. He made his place inside our house until John turned into a dad figure in our house.

He eventually began frequenting more and even started spending nights at our house. I was a child back then, so I couldn't exactly understand what was going on, but I started noticing changes. Like when John was around, my mom would cook special meals for him. She would clean his clothes and tidy up the place whenever John was to come.

Young as I was, I was able to notice that John was growing to become more than a friend to our family. I also remember being confused about which role he was trying to play. Say what you want, but children have strong intuition. They may not be able to add math problems up, but they can detect human problems and patterns. Annet had by then left us and went back to live with her family. So it was now me, Jeanne, my mom, and John.

One afternoon, my mom gathered my sister and me and said that she wanted to talk with us. She started by telling us how hard losing my dad been for her. Then she began to explain how important it is to have somebody like John in our lives. Support, somebody to lean on to, and to rely on a person. I quickly picked up what she is trying to mean. I right away asked her if she wants to replace my dad with John.

Do you think that was too wrong of me to be so straightforward, especially when she was trying to move her way around it gradually? Because I could see that as well. But I think it was not wrong, not like a child at least. Being a child sort of gives you the license to be blatant and straightforward. So I am not holding any guilt about that.

She was shaken and replied, saying, *"I am not trying to replace your daddy, but I also wanted to ask you guys' permission to have another man in my life. Wouldn't you be happy having somebody who would take you to visit kids in the village? Who will buy you clothes and food? Somebody who will take care of you like dad used to?"*

As a child, you are possessive about your parents. You may be thinking that I am giving too many justifications for being a child, but that is who I was then. One must be aware of how children are like, and if they must judge the kids, they must judge them accordingly. The only thought that ran in my mind back then was that my mom is trying to replace dad. And boy, I was not ready for it. So what do I do? I do what a typical child who realizes their one parent was replacing another does. I started crying instantly. I said no to my mom.

It was a 'No' to visiting the village with him, no to getting clothes by him, no to being taken care of like how dad used to do. I said no, and I was very serious about it. I knew that I could not stand somebody replacing my dad in our lives. And in that feeling, I found myself alone. On the other hand, my more mature sister Ange and my brother Lyan were more open about it. She welcomed the idea and was, in fact, very happy about it.

Perhaps any child living in conditions and circumstances we were living in, always on guard and on the move with no male adult around to care for them, would have been excited about that intervention. It meant having somebody to buy them what they want. It meant no regular starvation, and it meant a source of support and security. Where I could not see that, my elder sister Ange did.

At that moment, my mom first started realizing how starkly different I was, sort of like an odd one out in the family. She was taken aback when I started crying and screaming no at her gentle proposition. Then, of course, at the end of the day, I was not going to stop her from marrying John. Not having a husband, bearing a pregnancy alone, and having to take care of two daughters was a great burden - not the kind of task you want to see alone.

Also, she loved my father deeply, so in a way, she needed closure more than we did. I would not say she was so desperate for help because she did not run after John. He found her, liked her enough to keep coming back for her and proposed marriage. I reckoned that was why my mother voiced this decision out; it had his consent.

Things started to change since then. From that day on, John began to coming more often. He spent more nights in our house confidently without the need to lie to us where he slept. He had been secretive and considerate earlier about that, for he did not want us to think that he slept in the same bed with my mom. He also started acting more responsibly like a dad figure to us. He would not only buy us gifts but walk us around too. He treated all of us well. I also realized that my mom was always happy with him, which had been a rarity ever since the passing away of dad. It was easy to see my mom got over him and moved on soon. The best part was it was not because she was mentally ready to move on, but because it was the best thing she could do for us, for herself as a single mother with four young kids, living in a forest with wild animals. I was later grateful that my mom found somebody like John because once and a while we would all turn to find her scared to face darkness and animal sounds in the forest, without thinking that she would also get scared, I never thought of that!

In spite of the closeness, John was not always with us. He used to go for weeks and come back on his own, and initially, we did not know why. Later on, I learned that he was trying to collect information so that he could take us back to Rwanda. I still had not felt like considering John as my step-father. I would rather think of him as a family friend because that made more sense to me. You do not accept a person who has just been with you for a role that requires a lifetime to solidify. Days passed with our new conventions of family, and we eventually moved further into the woods.

We would just walk continuously for two days and end up somewhere in the middle of nowhere and station ourselves there. Apart from John, none of us were the best of navigators. I'm not sure if any of us, including my mom, knew which direction we were taking and where we were heading. There was only one thing we did know, and it was to keep our ears vigilant for anything regarding the bad boys, including rumors.

As long as my mom heard rumors that bad boys were lurking around for Rwandan blood, she would have us move as far as possible. One day, we moved into a forest that had very tall trees with monkeys all around. It was a queer place. We spent two days moving through it, and we could neither reach the forest's end nor find a suitable place to settle down. The food that we had carried with us was nearly ending.

The only thing that was remaining was sorghum flour, which my mom used for making porridge for our little brother Leo. We found ourselves too hungry and too tired to the point that we could not move any farther. Not only us children, but our mom, who was usually the more resilient one, also grew very tired. She had my young brother, Leo, at her back and my other young brother, Lyan, on her waist.

We sisters weren't free-handed either. We had huge bags containing everything we owned on our backs that were much larger than our tiny bodies. They were so huge that you would feel as if they were walking on their own; you would almost fail to notice the two girls carrying them. That was another one of the moments where my mom was afraid that we are finally going to die of hunger and thirst.

Imagine yourself in that state - though I would not wish it upon my enemies – where you could not speak or walk because no nourishment had gone inside your body. Our lips were cracked and dried white. Our eyes were heavy; our limbs were quivering. There came the point where I just had to lay down.

Everybody else followed. God bless my mom and her strength that she got back on her feet for our sake. It must be terribly hard to watch your children in that state and not to be able to do anything about it. So, my mom left us lying in the bushes while she crawled down the forest to find water. There was no river near our sight, not even a trickle or a gushing sound of it to indicate its presence. She still hoped to find one. God knows how we spent those two hours in the dangerous forest by ourselves.

We distracted ourselves from fears and hunger in those bushes. But two hours later, my mom returned with water. That was a sight to behold, an extraordinary moment. We were too weak to express it, but I am sure all us siblings were grateful for her. She brought us back from death.

We all got up when we saw her with the water, but she didn't directly give it to us. She mixed the cold water with sorghum flour that we had and helped us drink the porridge. It barely qualified as food, but it brought the energy back to our bodies. We could walk again. The forest is a very unsafe place to remain stagnant. There are wild beasts that may have eaten us had we stayed too long. So we were on the move once again.

Believe it or not, we walked another whole day on that diet. It seemed like we were surviving on our own prayers. Then, at approximately 9 PM, we finally saw something glimmer in the distance: A light that was coming from what appeared to be a house. You could not imagine our relief and excitement at that. It felt like we had won a million dollars or something. Such joy! We all clapped our hands and thanked God profusely that He finally led us to a place that showed signs of life. I remember looking at my mom and my sister, we all nodded at each other and wanted to stretch out smiles, but our mouths wouldn't budge. Only the shine in our eyes communicated a hint of a smile. Otherwise, we were too physically weak. I looked at my mom's face again and could see that it was lighter; it was as if a heavy load was taken off her. We were finally out of the terrific, labyrinthine forest.

We kept walking a few more miles to distance ourselves from the forest and to search for a safe place to lay our bodies down. We finally found a half-built abandoned house, isolated from others. When we neared it, it looked like no one has been in that house for years. It had bushes penetrating walls, tresses falling in from windows, and cobwebs dangling inside.

Yet, it was a sanctuary compared to sleeping outside, or, much worse, in the forest. The best part: we didn't sleep hungry that night. Around the house, there were wild banana trees, which my mom managed to get hold of. She also knew the technique to make fire. She aggressively rubbed two stones together. The pressure made them hot enough to spill out sparks until, finally, a marvelous mane of light and warmth we call fire burned before us.

That's how we used to make a fire in the forest, and before that in our various homes. So, we cooked the green bananas and ate them voraciously. If you think that was a relief, there was more awaiting us. After eating the bananas, we all contracted a terrible stomach-ache, probably because it had been three days since we had eaten anything, and the first thing we ate was not soft. Our stomachs had a hard time digesting it.

We spent a couple of weeks there in that house. Later, we also met a few people similar to us who needed shelter. They stayed around and offered, and in return for our kind gesture offered to take us where they usually get food from. We finally had a meal that comprised of something other than bananas. Fortunately, we had by then learned how to communicate in Swahili, which made it so more comfortable for us to talk to new people we met along the way.

All those who met us somehow parted happily and in good spirits. One morning, a lady who had agreed to take us to a place where they get food like yams and cassava roots from, came crashing to our place. She found our hospitality very heartwarming and, in return, insisted on taking my sister and me for gathering food. My mom was always afraid to leave us alone or with strangers, but the lady promised to take care of us. She was reluctant but complied, perhaps because the lady seemed to have that grandmotherly grace about her. My sister and I went with her, and she proved to be a good sport. But then, after walking for four hours, we crossed a very bridge called 'Ruhoro.' The bridge was made of strings for crossing and would swing back and forth as you walked on it. Imagine the dangling sensation on a bridge between two cliffs on a dizzying height.

Walking on, it felt like dying alive. Many thoughts about falling and that being the end of my life crossed my mind as I was only trying to imagine myself crossing the bridge. Without a doubt, it was the scariest bridge I have ever seen in my life. We knew that so many people had lost their lives on the Rohuro Bridge.

We had first resolved that we will not cross it, but again, the lady reminded us that our family is looking forward to the food we were bringing. Moreover, there was no other way around it. The only options we had were to either cross, die, or do not cross and allow our families to die. We ultimately decided to cross it. It must have been the longest time I had held my breath. My legs were jelly and stone hard at every other step as I tried to walk on planks thinner than sword's edge. Somehow, we finally made it to the other side carrying two big yams. I was little and had been too young to carry more than two yams because they were too huge and heavy. My mom had been anxiously waiting and thanked God when she saw us again. We narrated everything to her, the bridge, and crossing it with the weights and the risk.

She firmly stated that she wouldn't let us go there again. It was a decision that seemed so stern that it could have been in the constitution. But, of course, it did not work. We couldn't have lived without the food, and that turf had been our only resource. Over time, we made numerous other trips, over and over again. The Ruhoro Bridge became a child's play with all that crossing practice.

I cannot tell you what that place was where we were living, because I don't know. It was the middle of nowhere in the wild woods. We had completely lost contact with John since we had moved when he was not around, but he always found ways to find us. This time was no exception. Like the master navigator he was, he had found us yet again. After one month, we moved again near Bukavu, a big city in the Democratic Republic of Congo. We had then been, with passion, trying to find ways to get back to Rwanda. Our home – my home. John had some money, unlike my mom, and he found us a place to stay. It was a village, the kind of place where I hadn't visited before. It was my first time. There were so many bustling people around with this or that activities always going on. For me, it was a strange thing, more like a miracle. Coming from boring places with listless routines, I would spend my whole day watching people.

It felt amazing, and I would pray that I get to stay there a little longer. There came a time when I even thought that we had finally found a beautiful place to settle at, and we should probably find ways to go to school. However, yet again, I didn't know that it was also a temporary abode. It was a painful thought, as it had been a sort of painful nomadic life.

But the thought that we were moving intending to get back to Rwanda was comforting. We were, after all, going to our home where our origins were tied and emergent from. Despite our messed up and unstable life, or perhaps due to it, my mom's undying goal was to get us back to Rwanda, as soon as possible. We could start school then, like other kids. It had already been too late for my sister since she was seven and a half years old.

I was almost going to turn 6 in four months if I remember correctly. My mom told me she was trying to at least get us back to Rwanda in less than four months for my schooling's sake. I think she pushed us girls so hard for education because my mom was an educated woman herself. Not too qualified, but she had a high school diploma and knew the importance of education.

We stayed in Bukavu village for two months. I loved it there and made a few friends, but as I said, we, unfortunately, had to move again. John had gathered all the required information. He knew the way to Rwanda and how long it was going to take us to get there. He had memorized every single stop and how many nights we should spend where.

In short, he had everything mapped out to the last turn, even alternatives and precautions if things did not go as planned. He explained everything to my mom, and we were ready to go. Before leaving, I said goodbye to my temporary friends in the village, knowing full well that I will never see them again. I still told them that when I become rich, I will return to see them and be with them. But oh, those goodbyes were too painful! They gave us such an emotional farewell, tears leaking from every eye.

My mom had also made some friends there who offered us some food for our journey. They watched us as we left, waving with glistening eyes, not moving until we were entirely out of their view. I do not doubt that I had left a piece of my heart there behind. One thing that I have now realized was that almost everyone who met us loved my family. It is as strange as it is remarkable. We didn't have to spend an awful amount of time in one place to make friends. It was always easy for us to connect with people around and leave lasting impressions.

We then walked for three consecutive days before we finally reached our first stop, as per plan. There were houses around, and we spent a few nights in one or the other. They proved to be an appropriate resting place for gathering our energy and restocking ourselves. We would then head towards our next stop and spend more nights there, hoping to move again soon. Everything was going according to the plan by then, but we, unfortunately, had to stay a little longer. People around told us that the forest we were going to pass through had so many bad guys who eat and kill people – cannibals, yes.

Thus, we had to stay back until we could come up with another alternative. After much tries, nothing came up. In the end, John decided to go first and check if it was safe for us to follow him. He then went and never came back for three days. There did come the point when our fears made us think he was eaten and gone.

I later learned that he happened to come across the soldiers from Rwanda who was taking refugees from DR Congo back home. During the days he was gone, they had taken him as well, and he had no way to come back and let us know that it was safe. What were three days turned to a month; that's how long we stayed there. You can only imagine what would have become of our hopes, but life still goes on, in spite of the despair and uncertainty.

One morning, I was playing around and saw a troop of soldiers coming towards me. Terrified, I ran back and told my mom. The last thing I remember is that we were all surrounded by soldiers. They started questioning my mom, whose dress I was clinging onto tightly, and I thought they were going to kill us. In my heart, I knew this was the end, like with the Ruhoro Bridge.

We all huddled around mom, who was holding us all together as the soldiers ransacked our house. Upon their search of everything inside our cottage, they found my mom's High School diploma realized that she was a lost Rwandese Refugee. Honestly speaking, I had not known what kind of soldiers were they and what they wanted, but I didn't feel as bad about them as I did about those who murdered my father. I just know that they helped us as soon as they learned we were Rwandese.

Later that night, they brought us food, and I was so amazed by how nice they were to us. In my mind, soldiers equated to evilness and were bad men. Imagine the devil giving you sweets out of good heart, that's what it felt like. We, of course, took it because of hunger. Later on, I learned that they were Rwandan soldiers trying to get people back to the country. They told my mom to follow instructions and do everything they said. There was a determination in their eyes and face, and fear on my mother's. I could see how scared she was, her hopes sparse, especially in John's absence. I knew she was wondering how we were to survive this time.

After that night, the soldiers took us with them. They were very generous and kind-hearted to help my mom carry my brothers. Two of the soldiers carried my little brothers, trying to keep them engaged in the frantic situation. I was walking with one soldier holding my hand. Some of the instructions that they gave us were to follow them, not to look back or turn around if we find ourselves in the gun range.

There was no return from the journey we had set off. We were to continue moving unless and only if all soldiers turned around, which was very unlikely, they said. We followed all the instructions. All was going fine until we reached a place where we encountered a group of Congolese soldiers.

Without much thought, they opened fire on us. You can only imagine me and my siblings' alarm and agitation. Given my adventurous and hazardous life, it still had been the first time I was getting shot at. We were not supposed to turn around or back. I heard one commander saying that we should all duck and walk. It was a dangerous thing not to retreat and duck instead as if waiting for a lucky, or unlucky shot at finding us.

There was no end to those gunshots; they kept going on and on. Rat-tat-tat-tat and booms. Some soldiers died right there. I was getting tired of bending because my back hurt as I walked along, so I stood up a little. No sooner had I done that that one bullet nearly grazed my hair. I lost my mind at that. I knew that was a life or death moment. In a sense, that was my second life, yet it also seemed like we were just waiting for a bullet to come and lodge in us. Still, we could do nothing about it except pray in our hearts that some miracle happens.

At that moment, I did not know if my siblings or my mom were still alive since each of us was moving with a different group of soldiers. Plus, we were not allowed to look back. I kept my hopes that my family was still safe, but it also felt improbable, given the situation that we were in. As we continued to move on, our soldiers were even firing back upon the Congolese soldiers.

When I saw a bullet hit one of our soldiers and him falling, it hit me that I was in the middle of a war. The man was shot, but we carried on, no turning back and no looking around… just moving. Chaos is an understatement to describe that moment. Later on, we reached a massive building that appeared to be an abandoned church. We heard orders from the soldiers and commanders that we should go inside and seek refuge. I loyally followed everyone in front of me. We made it inside that hall, and instead of hiding, I found myself looking around to see if my mom and my sister made it. And then I saw both of them, and it felt that my heart had clicked back in place since the gunfire had separated us.

We were all still waiting on the other two soldiers who were carrying my two brothers. They also finally made it inside and couldn't help but thank God for that miracle. Can you imagine? Soldiers were dying around us; what were the chances all five of us could survive? It was unbelievable.

I looked at my mom, and my sister and gratitude spread across all of our faces. Though we all seemed very thankful, we couldn't smile. Anything could still happen. That church was no safe place. We huddled about our mom again, speechlessly, until we heard another instruction that we are going to spend a night there. The night went by so quickly as a blanket pulled from under someone's feet. It seemed like only a few minutes had passed and we hadn't slept enough. I woke up rubbing my eyes and hearing birds singing, the unmistakable sign of daybreak gracing. All of us needed to wake up immediately, and so we did. By the way, until that time, I had never seen let alone used a watch or a clock in my life. My mother may have before me, back in our homeland, perhaps, but never us. We relied on the sounds of the birds and the direction of the sun to know what time it was. Come to think of it; it really was a primitive yet natural way of living.

I have heard my mom saying that it is always midday, at 12 PM, when the sun is the strongest and heats your head directly from the top. Similarly, I could tell that it was around 4 PM when the sun was less intense and deviated away. She also said that it is always 5 in the morning when you hear the first bird singing, and they tend to stop their song tracks around 8 AM. So, that's how I grew up, without the concept of analog or digital time, just discerning via the changes in nature and the natural world around us.

If it is not so obvious already, let me tell you that the most concerning and significant times for us were the mornings, middays, and evenings; the time between that (10 AM or 2 PM) was something I never thought about nor heard my mom talk about. If you think these facts are shocking, consider this; we would also every night check for the weather next day by approximating the number of stars we have in the sky and by also assessing the cloud direction. My mom would teach us that the following day will be sunny if we have numerous stars in the night sky before the day. She told us that it would be rainy if we have no stars in the sky. How is that possible, you might think? Common sense, the sky would be covered by the clouds. She also used to specify that it will rain in the later afternoon in case there are few stars visible, mixed with light clouds or mist.

I believed in my mom's weather forecasting skills for most of her weather predictions used to turn out correct. She was a witch. I used to think she was a genius in my mind. Early in the mornings too, she would wake up, stand akimbo, look up and squint at the sky, scrutinizing it, and conclude about the day's weather depending on how the number of clouds in the sky and the wind direction

So, yes, once again, it was a natural order of living.

Out of inspiration, I would sometimes too try to predict the next day's weather and eagerly ask her if I'm correct or wrong. She would be very patient with me. I remember she used to say to me that I have to put consideration into the flow of the wind as well. No matter how cloudy it looks –

and this could be priceless knowledge for you too, dear reader – if the wind is too much, there is a high chance that it will not rain. We may not have known the science behind it, the inner workings and mechanisms that run behind the entire system, but we arranged things widely given our circumstances.

As it went, I got used to checking for the next day's weather every single night. It became like a routine before our bedtime. Where other children far, far away would say their prayers or floss their teeth, we used to read the book of the skies. Sometimes, believe it or not, we would even name the stars! This one particular star, we used to call *Kibona Umwe,* which means only one person could see it.

The reason behind this was that it used to materialize like a flash, *whoosh,* or *twinkle*; however you prefer it, but you could see it just once, and it would disappear right away, even before I could call my siblings to come and see it. And similarly, before they could call me so that I could observe it. We never saw it together, and I know when you hear it like that, it sounds more like an illusion, but we know what we saw. It was a special star to us that made us delighted amid even a boring night.

My mom once said to us that whenever you see it, make a wish right away before it vanishes. *"That wish will become true,"* she told us. Every night I would eagerly wait for that special star, for *Kibona Umwe,* and make my wish. And yes, my wish was what you must be predicting too it was. It was the only big wish I had at that time: to find myself back in Rwanda.

I didn't ask for my father back, not for flashy clothes and savory foods, but only for Rwanda, the beautiful place that only existed in my imaginary world. The child that I was, I also kept a list of everything I would do once I get there. I would see *Kibona Umwe* a few times every week, and I would continue to make the same wish over and over again. You may call that naivety or whatever, but that was hope for me and a symbol of the divine too.

Apart from *Kibona Umwe,* there were other special stars for me, too. For instance, the star that would be bigger than the rest of the stars would occupy a special place for me. Whenever I would observe one of those in the night sky, I would immediately call upon my siblings as well as my mom to come and stare at it together with me. Watching and counting stars became a big part of my family. It was like a nightly ritual, a custom. It was one of the few things in those days that used to give me so much joy as a child. I didn't have many other exciting things happening in my life as a five-year-old, yet I knew my childhood was different. It constituted a life of the wilderness, firstly a world that was separate from the world of those children that live in either cities or villages. On top of that, I was in a world of my own, too. It was inside my head.

I never had anyone to play with besides my sister. However, she also acted like another adult due to the responsibilities on her shoulders. That was my life. I could only wish I had friends, and I had hope that one day, I will be able to have friends to play with. I guess one benefit that this gave me was imaginary friends. I used to talk to myself a lot, entertaining myself with my imaginary friends.

I would greet them every morning and ask them how they are doing and when they will be coming to visit me. As abnormal as it sounds, having imaginary friends was something that made me feel normal. It was always a good feeling to be talking to myself. It even now gives a sense of self-dependence. Psychologically speaking, these days of our childhood are what form us. Having had too much dependence on friends and affluent parents who fulfilled my every wish would have made me into a stubborn and non-introspective. You might wonder that this makes me lack in social skills, such as humor, well, you have another surprise coming. I would make jokes with my friends and laugh with and at them, acting, and making myself believe that it was one of my friends who is making me laugh. It fueled my imagination and fantasy-prone nature.

At the end of every conversation with my imaginary friends, I would say goodbye to them and pretend to hug them (in truth, hugging myself). Deep down, I knew I was lonely, and that I had no friends, but I hoped that I would have them someday. Besides, I at least had self-love.

I once asked my mom what it feels like to have friends and what friends do for each other. She would be caught off guard, yet would try to explain to me by telling us her childhood stories with her best friends. That would comfort me, too, and give me hope. I loved my mom's stories. It was one of the only things that would make me sit with her every day whenever she used to be cooking. She would tell us stories of her family and her siblings, minding the pot with her eyes glazed. She would narrate to us about her brothers and uncles and that we should call them *Tonto* once we meet them. While her sisters, our aunties, we should call them *Tantine*. I remember how fervently I memorized those names and anticipate the days that I would have to use them regularly, especially *Tantine*, for it sounded fancier to me.

Early that morning, we woke up and continued our journey with the soldiers. There was one soldier whom I was walking with, and he was telling me different stories of what other kids of my age do in Rwanda. In his melodic tone, he assured me that we will get there safely, have a good life and that I will be able to make friends. There was something about his reassurance that I haven't forgotten till today. He definitely made me feel content with his words.

Before we reached our destination, which was the city of Goma, I had been getting used to being around these soldiers men we were walking with. They were kind people who used to feed us yellow corn and rice. They were the ones who introduced me to the taste of rice for the first time. I was instantly in love with it. It was like a luxury in my mind, and I would imagine how pleasant things would be if I could eat rice every day. It was the most delicious meal I had tasted in my five years of life on earth. Then, in the end, the kind rice-feeding soldiers had to part form us. They were only supposed to, and, I guess, instructed to take us to Goma, which had a refugee camp that was receiving Rwandese people. Its function was temporary. The camp hosted the refugees only temporarily before they would be taken back to Rwanda through the UN Refugee Agency, called UNHCR. We spent another five nights along the way, which constituted a long but pleasant journey before we reached Goma.

It was a huge city and was closer to Rwanda and the Democratic Republic of the Congo border. It was around 7 pm when we reached there. I was watching what a big city looks like for the very first time. First the rice and then this, it was a time of my firsts. I saw bright lights all around the roads and houses; everything was illuminated and seemed like a fairy tale to me.

I could not believe what my eyes were seeing. Electricity was a stranger to me, and so were lights. We had always been living under the light of candles or oil lamps. Full of curiosity, I asked my mom how those bright lights functioned. I guess she, too, was surprised to realize that I had never seen lights. Yet she replied gently, saying, *"That works on electricity that runs through those wires and powers them up. You will see many of them even when we get home, to Rwanda.* " A few minutes later, I was looking at something moving swiftly with people inside it. I was then completely sold out by it and so star-struck that something like that could exist. My mom held me by the shoulders and dragged me back, pushing us both away from the roads to the roadside. She calmly but cautiously explained that it was a car, and it carries people to places in a quicker time than we travel on foot. Me being a kid, and that too a curious one, I had so many questions running through my head like a current.

How does it move? What makes it move? Where are the people sitting? Does it feel comfortable? Does it hurt? Is it fun? What if it falls or slides? What about when it is raining, does it slide then? How does it take you to your destination, and how does it know where you are going? What is it made up of? Does it speak or listen? What if you want to turn, how do you communicate with it? And on they went, as I said, like a current. I was filled with questions, and my mom couldn't provide all the answers. If you think I was the only culprit of mom's headache, you have a thing coming.

My siblings were no lesser flabbergasted. They were also asking as many questions as I was. We felt as if we are in some different realm; it was not the world of jungles or villages we were accustomed to. I just kept watching how cars moved and the zipping wind that gets to you when a car passed by. And how away it would go, blurring and then vanishing into the distance.

And so many colors! It always felt like the car could just turn and hit me off and away from the roadside to somewhere. It was the best experience and the most fantastic thing I have ever seen. I was speechless and amused. It made me believe that there must be things out there that could fly.

A few minutes later, a motorcycle passed by, and I thought it was just a fancy bicycle since I had seen some bicycles in one of the small cities we had been to along the way. Yet, I was still surprised by how fast it moved and how much noise and smoke it leaves in its wake compared to a bicycle. I, later on, I learned that a motorcycle was different from a bicycle. Probably sensing that it was something she should have earlier done, my mom tried to educate us as much as she could about everything. Not only did she explain the things we had been seeing, but also the things we were to see. But then, it was just too much information to take in one night, and mom was tired too. We arrived at the refugee camp within Goma around 9 PM. There were many other refugees and refugee families over there with a lot of kids around. I felt so much joy upon seeing kids. It elated be, and I wanted to hold them or at least speak to the ones who were of the same age as me.

Alas, there was no time for socialization. We had to go directly to the refugee camp managers, and my mom had to fill out some papers. Then they started asking her things orally too. There were different questions. Which part of Rwanda was she from? How long has she been out of the country? Then, we were given corn flour, which was the leading refugee food along with beans, corn, and vegetable oil.

Following that, the soldiers who had brought us there had to go back. I knew the hour of separation had to come, but I had still grown sad. I'm not sure where they went, but they had to go to their duties to make sure that we are all set. We had formed a special connection, and it was hard saying goodbye to them. These were the people who had been strangers more than a week ago. They, too, had grown to like us so much, and it showed on their faces. In spite of them being military men, they revealed their emotions to us and gave us good wishes. They treated us so well for the whole time we had been with them. I was surprised, pleasantly, however, at one gesture. The soldier who had been with me the whole time, like a bodyguard, gave me a tight hug. He wished goodbye to me and prayed for my safety.

I asked him if I will ever see him again, and right there, I wanted to cry. He replied that we would meet in Rwanda and ruffled my hair. The other soldier was no less of a sweetheart. He was the one who was had been walking with and protecting my mom. He said goodbye to her, with the same sincerity a son says to her mother, and he gave her some money too.

We all thanked them for being so kind to us. Such goodwill was as rare as was precious in my life. It was my first time seeing soldiers who were so helpful and kind. Ever since my father's murder, I had begun to fear soldiers. That experience, thus, was a lesson in life — a lesson for open-mindedness and not generalizing using one mere example. Following their departure, the refugee manager gave us some toiletries as well, such as a few bars of soaps and a

Vaseline. I was used to going on for days without a proper shower with soap and all, given the circumstances. In fact, it had been almost a year since I used an actual soap if I remember correctly. We did, however, have a makeshift soap, you could say. There was this plant whose name I cannot remember. My mom knew that it produced foam when you squeezed it in your hand.

That foamy plant used to help us manage our showers. It acted as our soap, and fortunately, that plant was present almost everywhere in the forest. We didn't even have to carry it around. We just used to go looking for it every time we would camp somewhere. In that regard, if you count that as cleaning and cleansing, then perhaps I will say that it hadn't been a year since I had used soap.

Moreover, taking a shower for me meant finding a nearby river and rinsing myself thoroughly, not once but a couple of times while using that foam-producing plant. (It would have been so convenient if I could remember its name). So that was a substitute for soap. On the other hand, we had no Vaseline or body lotion in all our traveling periods. The last time I used Vaseline was when my daddy was still around. He used to buy some for us to help us moisturize and take care of our bodies. But when the manager brought it to us, I had gone months without moisturizing my body, and yes, I'm not shy to say, I had basically gotten used to it. The refugee camp took us around, showing my mom where we will be sleeping. It was a gigantic hall with no mixed-sex residence. Every room was supposed to be either only for females or for males.

Rather, women had one entire hall to themselves, and men had another. But because my brothers were too little, and the managers understood our situation, they were allowed to sleep with us. We were all given one mattress. There wasn't custom for privacy in that place. Everybody could literally see everybody in the hall, sleeping like dead bodies, save for the noise of the crying kids, which went on 24/7.

It was one of the things I had to get used it, and eventually, my ears were immune to it. I had been through worse things, anyway. That first night we didn't make any meal. They provided us with ready-to-eat cornflour paste along with beans. It tasted pleasant to my taste buds, primarily because it was well prepared with some oil in it, which was another something I was deprived of. Oil, too, was something I hadn't tasted for months. And then, of course, us being indigenous folks, we did not know how to use eating utensils such as spoons and folks either. Thus, we didn't even bother trying our hands at it. We just washed our hands like we used to, and got right to it, good ol' traditional style eating. One thing my mom had taught us, and I have mentioned this before, too, was never to take food from strangers. And strangers included everybody else except my mom and my siblings.

So basically, we were not allowed to eat any food that is not coming from my mom's hands without her permission. And as that went, even when the refugee manager offered us dinner, we initially refused to have it. Our pangs of hunger were carving a hole inside us. We were all staring at our mom, and the food was waiting in all its delicious glory.

What can I say, Mom's permission was a prerequisite before eating. Moreover, this strategy of hers was a form of protecting us from any food poisoning since we lived with people who were strangers, and they did not seem to like us. Better safe than sorry, you know. In fact, before my daddy died, my mom was poisoned by their Congolese, right where we used to live.

She had almost died following my dad's death, so from that time, we had to be very careful. It did not hurt to be safe in that case. My mom had managed to convince us that people don't like us and that they wanted to kill us. *"That's why we lived in isolated places most of the time,"* she would say. It was somewhat true because Rwandese were being hunted in the Democratic Republic of Congo at that time, and we very much looked like Rwandese.

Plus, we spoke Kinyarwanda, the official language of Rwanda. The following morning, my mom showered us with soap and oiled our bodies with Vaseline that was part of our quota. It made us feel cleaner than we had ever been our entire life. And so fragrant too, that for the first time, I felt inclined to obsess over myself profusely.

After that, she went to the market and bought bread and rice from the money the soldiers gave. As part of our safety regime, she instructed us to stay inside the sleeping hall anytime she is not around. We obeyed our mom, faithfully. Well, faith wasn't the only factor; it was a matter of pain too. If we hadn't obeyed without protest to her and misbehaved instead, we knew we were in for a spanking. So, nope, never would take that risk. After she returned home, she found us right where she had instructed and suggested. Nodding to us, she went into the kitchen, made porridge from the cornflour that she was given, and we ate it together. The bread went deliciously well with the porridge. The combination, which I was trying for the first time, tasted like heaven to me. I couldn't imagine how food could get any better than that. I would perch the scrumptious gooey liquid with the warm crusty bread, put it in my mouth, and everything would dissolve in the background. My eyes would be closed with the dream-coming-trueness of it all.

My mom showed us this technique of eating bread and porridge. Not only that, she taught us all the etiquettes of eating among respectable people. From the way we sit while eating to the way we chew our food with mouths closed, to the manner of not talking while food is in the mouth (*"You first have to swallow it all the way down before speaking,"* she would say), she taught us everything.

She also taught us that once we are done eating, the ideal thing is to lie down for three to five minutes so that your food can go to the stomach. I once asked her why we had to lie down since the food goes in the stomach right away. She responded that if you start doing physical activities right away after eating, your food will rise and come out as puke. *"Since it is always stuck in the throats, lying down helps carry the food to the stomach for digestion,"* she had patiently informed. I grew up believing this theory of lying down a few minutes after eating. It made all the sense to me, but mom could never convince my other siblings of that. I guess I too adopted this practice after I vomited once because of jumping around right away after eating.

After that, she instructed all of us to lay down for a few minutes. It was night time. Now that I think about it, I think it was also a sly way to get us children to bed right away after dinner. None of us siblings were easy ones at that. We always used to give our mother a hard time.

During the noontime after the porridge breakfast, my mom happened to prepare some rice with beans. Given how heavy porridge and bread was, I was by no means expecting any other meal. I thought it would make me go the whole day, so you can imagine my surprise and resistance to have my lunch. I guess it's important to mention that the richness of porridge and bread was not the only reason. I was the reason too. You know about my past, the circumstances that I had come from, so it only made sense that my appetite was used to one meal per day or no meal at all for days. When my mom said that we would be eating again at noon, I was a little confused, but, and this part may shock you, I was also delighted. I could see my life-changing day by day for the better. Who thought I could be eating two times a day? Or eating bread and rice? This was my idea and experience of luxury at that tender age. Believe me or not, these were things I never imagined nor expected to have. I was very excited for every new day, knowing that I will at least have two cooked meals.

Back in the forest, we were used to roasting almost everything but yams. Mostly, and once in a while, we satisfied ourselves with green bananas. Those were our typical everyday meals. On top of that, we had no cooking pots or cans and were always uncertain about finding water at the time of need. Thus, roasting was easy and the most convenient option at that time in the past. Those days at the camp, we had no issue arrange either of the two options above mentioned. If you think that is surprising, get this. We all subsisted with having about two to three outfits in our non-existing closet. I had two dresses, and I used to wear one of those for at least two months.

We used to wash them down by the river on sunny days so that we could also dry them right away. But that deprivation of our life was changing. Our whole lifestyle was changing in the camp if you think about it. After spending and relaxing for two days at the camp, my mom went back to the market and bought us all new pairs of clothes from the money she had received. I now had a new dress in my non-existing closet – or should I say in my two-outfit closet.

My sister and brothers each got one outfit, too, and for herself, my mom bought a long skirt and shirt. I was right away ready to jump into my new outfit. Once I did, it felt so good! The feel of having new clothes was a strange feeling for me. I felt clean and pristine in them. Mom did not have enough money to buy us shoes, and she apologized for that.

I mean, I didn't mind, because in my six years of living I have never worn shoes. I was used to walking and running around bare feet; however, my soles had become hard and callous because of walking miles every day. Though I did not have a particular desire for it, when I saw people around wearing nice clothes and shoes, I caught on that wish that I had shoes too. I know many people could not relate to this kind of yearning because of the circumstances they were raised in. I am not ignorant enough to know my upbringing came in an environment of extreme deprivation. But I'm sure where luxury and convenient lifestyles exist, there also exist people who had an upbringing in worse conditions than me. I want to let you know that my heart goes out to all of you. I have been in your shoes, and you mine. I know how this living feels like.

So, at that point of envy and yearning too, I comforted myself with not overthinking about it. I understood that I should be thankful for even having good meals and not sleeping outside. My situation was much better than where and what I had come from the camp. In my family, none of us had any shoes, and that includes my mom.

Yet, mom promised to buy us some when we get to return home, back in Rwanda. I liked the idea of having my first shoes ever, the ones I could call mine back at home. One day just to see what it was like to wear shoes, I asked to borrow one shoe from a kid who seemed to get along with my family most of the time. The two of us agreed that I would wear the shoe for one minute and then give it back to her. She raised her leg up to her hip, pulled it off, and handed me her flip flop shoe to lend.

I carefully slipped my feet into it, and the first thing I noticed was that it added some inches to my height. Yes, just wearing one shoe did that. For the most part, however, wearing the shoe felt uncomfortable to me, ironically. Again, that was because I was used to the opposite, i.e., not wearing any footwear. So, I gave it back to her before the end of the minute. After three weeks at the refugee camp, I was already getting used to having a normal life.

Even this normalcy was a relative one, because refugee life was, technically speaking, not a really good life. We still had deprivations of food from time to time, and diseases lurked around if you weren't too careful. But we had a roof over our head, and it was better than walking all day in burning forests and sleeping in bushes with insurmountable hope that a snake doesn't bite you.

In the camp area, there also was a church where refugees used to go to pray. I would say that there is always a church, or I guess more of the times, near refugee camps. It would be a fair thing to say that the refugees are the most prayerful people. My mom is also one of the most religious people I know – if that doesn't already prove from the blind hope she had in God and for our future. She loved the church so profusely. She would take us there every Sunday, and we would usually comply happily. The pastor at the refugee camp would mention that we need to pray for the upcoming trip. That was the trip of going back to Rwanda. Praying to God meant speeding up the process, which, by that time, had already taken longer than we were told and had expected. Some people we spoke to told us they have been at the camp for two months.

In a refugee camp, this knowledge is available by the amount of radiance and hope in people's faces. The ones who have been there for more extended periods have dim hope. They told us that it could even take three months before we are taken back to our home country. Us being us, we held our hopes high throughout.

My mom would mention every day that we are going home soon. *"Just a few more days and we'll see the greens of our land and the welcoming arms of our people,"* she would say. My everyday fantasies were all about Rwanda. I used to imagine how rich and beautiful Rwanda will be. I wondered if the city of Goma was as beautiful as my home. That is true, the city of Goma gave me a decent premise, as well as to my imaginations.

I used to wonder how bigger the roads and cars would be in Rwanda, and how fancier and taller every building will be compared to in Goma; how radiant and generous the lights and people would be. I fantasized so much about Rwanda basing it all on Goma city that I even used to think the sky would be different than it was above us at the camp. I would also imagine that I will never touch soil nor dirt again in Rwanda.

It was a pristine city inside my head, one where I could walk happily shoeless, with my feet never, ever getting dirty. Wearing shoes over there would be a mere formality in my head. I also couldn't wait to get there so that I can finally start school. It has been my dream to go to school. I loved the idea of education and learning about so many unknowns like cars and flashing lights and astounding buildings.

I imagined other friendly six-year-old children in the same class as me, all looking jolly and eager. Every night I would pray that I wake up to find the UNHCR car parked outside to take us home finally. This would be the first thing I would do every morning - not brush my teeth, not sort out my hair, just spring off the bed and run out the camp full of vigor, and hope to find that beautiful white car with blue writing that everybody talked about. I would always wake up to an empty space where the UNHCR car should have been. After the passage of a month where the familiarity with the place and people had risen to new heights, the talks around the camp went that the UNHCR car will finally be arriving that week to take us to our home country. It wasn't like all those other unreliable talks with one or two whispers here and there.

It was authentic for it had come from the refugee camp manager, and everyone was talking about it. The excitement was so high that we could have thrown a party if we had the resources. Gratitude had taken over us, yet after all our months-long patience, we couldn't wait for the auspicious day. The preparations were underway all around the camp. In our family, we started washing our clothes and packing whatever little stuff we had.

Not only clothes-wise, but we were preparing appearance-wise too. My mom bought a pair of scissors and shaved our hair so that we can look clean when we get home. She, on the other hand, had long natural hair, which she began combing regularly. The refugee camp manager kept going around all the time, asking everyone to be ready and have their things packed. He would be sure to warn us that we had to be punctual and prepared and that we all had to stay at the refugee camp, or otherwise, we would be left behind. This was all about the things that were surrounding me. I haven't yet begun to tell you what I was feeling. The home I had dreamed of all my life was one step closer to me. It all depended on that van to finally take us away, and even that moment was nearing. And how do I tell you what I was feeling inside me? It was ineffable.

If there is one word for that feeling, it would be delirium. But if we are going to be exact about it, I was a little nervous, anxious, and happy. Rwanda was like a land in a fairy tale world. A mythological country, a fantasy. It, of course, was going to be large, and became even larger in my mind, for we didn't know exactly which part of Rwanda we were going to.

All I knew was that we were going home, a home I had always dreamt about. The time came for instructions. My mom's directive voice came, and in an instant, we gathered in one room, all eyes on her. She elaborately detailed us on the nitty-gritty like usual. She said that we are going to the place where she grew up, where she and her parents used to live. She had no idea who might possibly be there or if their house is still standing. She gave us the heads up about that, which denoted that we had to be prepared that we might be on our own in Rwanda. But if we did find someone from her relatives or family, whoever it was, we had to be very respectful and composed.

This changed something in me. In all my fantasies of, for, and about home, I never entertained the idea of what it will be like for mom to return to the village where she grew up. How will people greet her, how will she act with them, whether she would be emotional, whether they would be cold to her; all these questions raced in my head. I couldn't help but worry about all of this, especially since her family hadn't seen her ever after she got married.

So, this is what I knew. My mom grew up in a small village called Vunga, in a massive family of twelve children. The financials weren't much of an issue because they had support for their number of members, but this was because her family was considered to be one of the wealthiest families in the whole village. Her daddy owned the biggest restaurant there and not only made a lot of money compared to others but also gave employment opportunities for the people in his village. For that reason, he had respect too. He had managed to educate his children, my mom included, which was as big a deal in the village as it was rare. Everyone feared families with educated children. That's an aspect of education; it equips you with the critical thought to look underneath the status quo and wrongdoings in society. Add to that, my mom was among the brightest kid in her family, and she had gone to the best school for high school.

Her love for education was such that she did not stop just there. Later, she got a teaching high school diploma and got employed at a school right away. Given the primitive life they led in the village, the teachers were the most highly paid employees, and teaching jobs were much respected. So, like father like daughter, my mom had a pretty good reputation around the place and earned well.

After getting her first teaching job, her paths crossed with my daddy (May his soul Rest in Peace), who was working for the largest beverage manufacturing company in Rwanda. Its name was Bralirwa and was renowned as a beverage distributor. Then, as relationship stories go, they fell in love and got married. After my mom and daddy's marriage, they moved to Kigali city. That was where my daddy used to live.

Everyone in the village knew my mom due to her success in the teaching field and her ostentatious wedding. It is known that she had the most beautiful wedding in the whole village because both were rich parties and did not shy away from spending on a grandiloquent event. Add to that, she was educated too and was marrying an educated person. I can imagine it to be as close to aristocratic as it could be.

I am fortunate that my parents were both academically gifted, my daddy more than my mommy. Yes, you read that right. He was the smartest student and used to hold the number one position throughout high school, as he used to tell me. My parents' success was every parents' wish for their kid in Vunga village.

They would hold the couple as an exemplar and motivate their own children using their example. My mom and daddy lived happily for the first year of their marriage. They saw the time of their life. She would not stop talking about the happiness and the relationship being at the prime with a luxurious yet humble lifestyle governing everything. If you ever had the chance to sit with my mom, she would nonstop talk about the beauty of those days.

She would tell you about their visits to expensive hotels and night clubs. Her eyes would glaze over thinking about the different beverages dad used to bring home every night. But they were not selfish in their lifestyle. Mom tells me she would give some beverages to their neighbors and help the poor regularly. And then there was music. My parents loved music so much that they had one big radio and speakers installed in the house, to which they would dance almost every day.

But then came the civil war, and my parents tasted the bitter truth of the statement that happy days rarely last longer. Given all this, when I reflect on how miserably mom spent her days during and before that refugee period, my eyes tear up. My heart stammers in its beat, and my eyes bow down to the ground.

She used to live the life of a queen, but in my childhood, she was reduced to a servant. Probably worse. I felt so bad for my mom; I still do. She did not deserve all that transpired with her! But not all hope was lost. Back in the camp, burgeoned on hope. My mom had kept her high school diploma, which was the only thing that she could move with almost everywhere. She told us that once she gets back home, she will acquire a job and be able to afford to give us the life we had been deprived of. She would buy us shoes and beautiful clothes, and we'd have nutritious meals to eat, she would tell us. Now, back then, we didn't know what a high school diploma was precisely, but the way she talked about it, we knew that it was the most valuable thing that my mom possessed. And we knew that it would get her a job and our lifestyle would improve.

That's all we needed to know anyway. It made us pass our days dreamily even. And just like that, the week went by without much of an itch. And bravo! UNHCR truck finally arrived! We danced on the streets ecstatically, and I too rejoiced without holding anything back. It was the day I had been waiting for my whole life.

The truck was the medium of my journey back home, and the bridge for the route back home was repaired. I was beside myself with joy and so was my family. I couldn't wait to get inside the truck. It may come as a dismay to some, or not if you are reading me avidly, but that was going to be my first car ride ever. As happy we had been, the situation became riotous when the time came to step inside the truck. Getting inside was such a fight, and everybody was bottlenecking through since the huge truck appeared small, given how many families were there. It was a scene of an apocalypse, the commotion, the congestion, the chaos of one-upping others. So, our family wasn't going to hold back either. We had to fight for it, but we eventually got in.

Here's another thing about my mom; she has always been very energetic and a fighter. She managed to push and squeeze through the crowd deftly, with us all glued to her like mice to cheese. Add to that; we were carrying all our belongings with us. Once inside, our celebrations were only inside because of the number of people left behind and fear of what was coming.

We sat there still, quietly waiting for the car to start moving. The car was filled beyond its capacity, it felt, the kids around us were crying, as usual, the smell of odorous body was wafting around the cargo that seemed small. It was my first car experience, and things were not looking pretty, given the car had not even begun moving. I did everything not to fear that my experience of Rwanda was going to be disappointing too. I was impatiently waiting for it to start moving. Every sensation I was feeling was a new experience for me, save for my feet bare on the ground, shoeless.

I was grateful that my mom had picked a relatively nice spot for us. We sat close to the car window so we could have something to hold on to, whether it be the views outside or the railing; figurative or literal. My mom told us that that we would need to hold on very tightly to either the window or the railing or each other otherwise, we would fall, and people will step on us. That was what her worried voice uttered once the car started moving.

My mom repeated *"hold tight,"* and no sooner, I had started feeling dizzy and nauseous. When I looked outside, it was like everything in motion, be it the trees or cars or the houses, it was a scary sight. It was supposed to comfort me, I thought. I was to hold on to it for the rough ride figuratively.

Not a kilometer away, I had a piercing stomachache, and all of a sudden, I started throwing up. My mom, much to my surprise yet so mindful about everything seemed prepared for it. She handed me a piece of cloth, and I threw up neatly enough that nobody else was affected by it. But it was draining. I was left with almost no energy to stand, and so my mom laid me down and covered my eyes so that I won't be able to look at anything outside again.

I still remember that dizzying nausea; it was like my brain was not registering nor accepting that I should take deep breaths and remain calm. It was like being on a merry-go-round that was not stopping. What scared me was watching everything move, but it wasn't that anything was moving; we were just moving past everything. Talk about late and untimely discoveries, heh?

My first car experience equated with the worst that could ever be. My expectations had been opposite, and here I was, suffering the cruelty of a hysterical mind. I wanted the car to stop because I was feeling terribly sick. Blood pressure was down, the heart was flat, and the eyes fluttery and half-close. Breathing became an alien concept, and the stifling bodies did nothing to help. It felt like I was put suddenly in a matchbox. That's what the ventilation was also like.

If you think that surprises you, you have another thing coming, as had I. Opposed to me, my sister seemed to be enjoying the ride, full of rapture and awe. But then my two young brothers were screaming and crying deafeningly, which made me feel as if the roof of the bus would blow away from the pressure. One of them was throwing up as well. My mom had yet again to act like a machine, a superheroine to save us all. It was a lot for her to handle, but thank God that my older sister was feeling good and was able to support my mom with our luggage that we had to hold for the entire trip as there was no space for luggage. I don't know how it would seem to you, but one of the comforting things for me was that I was not the only one who was sick, not just in my family but in the whole truck.

Many kids and adults were throwing up and screaming too. I, fortunately, was mature enough not to scream. The other half was the only thing I need to work on. It took us approximately one hour to get to the border of Rwanda and DR Congo. I thought the car would make a stop, but it did not stop there. We continued moving until we reached the Nkamira refugee camp.

It was another Rwandan refugee camp that collected Rwandan refugees and took them to their local destinations in their homeland. As for me, who first was clueless about our destination, I now started thinking we will go directly to my mom's village. But that was not the case. It was that other refugee camp we were fated to stop and stay at for a while. I remember it was a September evening when we reached the Nkamira refugee camp and stepped out.

What surprise it was when I later learned that we had entered Rwanda. Why? Because it didn't seem like it. There was still barrenness, wilderness, same devastated faces, and nothing new, no freshness in the air. It was Rwanda, I learned, and seemed nothing like how I imagined it would be. But then it was supposed to comfort me that we were not at the heart of our home, for it was just another refugee camp.

I asked my mom where we were, and she was careful to explain that even though we were now in Rwanda, we were not exactly at the place where we're supposed to settle. All that my adamant brain took from that was that we were not yet home. The Nkamira refugee camp was more like a transit camp center and was not in the city as the previous refugee camp in Goma.

Once again, I felt like I had not yet stepped in Rwanda because my objects of fancy were nowhere to be seen. Where were all the beautiful roads and buildings I had in my mind? Where were the deluxe cars? I held on to my hopes like a stubborn child that once we get to where we are supposed to settle, everything will be different. All the luxuries will be there, and that would be when I will be able to see the Rwanda I have dreamed about. I had created a fairytale home in my mind and wasn't going to be let down by the first blow that threatened the foundations of my fantasy. My eyes were not ready to receive anything I did not have in my imagination, unless, of course, it was better than what I had in my imagination. So, with the will still strong, with hopes regathered, I was still waiting to get home, excited, and nervous. At the camp, as per regular protocol, we went through the typical process of checking in where we were supposed to be given food such as rice, oil, corn, beans, and toiletries.

The first comfort after reaching the first stop, as you might have guessed, was that we had rice. I loved that they gave us rice! At the previous camp I had eaten it for the first time and since then too only a few times. Yet, here it was again. And how pleasant it was to have rice at the new place.

I guess one of the pleasant and reassuring things in migration is when a happy or comfortable experience of a previous place synchronizes with another of the second place. A week into Nkamira transit camp passed by pretty slowly. My mom shared more stories about her and daddy's history. Meanwhile, the officials informed us that we would be taken to our destinations in two days, so we needed to get ready again. The same atmosphere that was weaved in Goma camp during the last days took over again. Or, I don't know, was supposed to. The UNHCR truck was expected to carry us back home as usual, but I now had questions in my mind about where we will be going. Along with hope, fear had set its camp in my heart, too, after learning that my mom and daddy used to live in Kigali city before the political instability, which led them to move. I asked my mom if they had a house in Kigali. They did not.

Unfortunately, they were renting. However, my daddy was planning to build one in the same year they moved. I held my hopes high that we will be going to see our relatives along with Rwanda, my homeland, which I have been waiting to see. Struggling and suffering throughout living a nomadic life, I thought all worries would be over once home sweet home appears before me and carries me in its arms.

On the day the truck was to come to pick us up again, my mom had bathed us and oiled our tiny bodies with Vaseline. It was like the first time, only, this time, I was prepared for nausea, and it was not going to be my first car ride either. She had instructed us anew and prepared us with the provisions for the next long journey. I remember we looked and smelled good, all of us in our new outfits, which mom had purchased previously. I had on a mid-sized colorful dress whose exact color I don't recall. It was the same dress I wore when we were coming from Goma to Nkamira city. In the mirror, I saw a girl who looked very skinny and tall, full of hopes and excitement that glimmered on her face as she waits for the next chapter of her life to open.

The only nervousness I had at that time was about the truck ride. I had begun dreading riding in the car, which was something I had become excited about in my mind. Given how bad my first experience was, I told my mom that I had become less interested in car rides. Mom comforted me. She was prepared for anything that can happen to us throughout the journey, such as getting sick, scratched, or hurt. She is always prepared for the worst, and I love that about her.

The truck came, and we were no longer dancing, in spite of the joy and hope within. It was time to say goodbye to refugee camps, and as a tribute to reconciling with my past and moving on, I threw my old torn skirt away. *"Goodbye, old life,"* the gesture seemed to say. I knew I was not going to wear that long-kept dress again, for I was expecting new clothes that may come from our relatives or my mom's friends. Being a kid of five, I was full of expectations. We got the update that the truck was not going to take us exactly where we were supposed to reside, given that there was no direct nor paved road to the place where my mom grew up. Hence, we had to get off somewhere close and walk the remaining distance. Someone told us it was going to take two hours. I had no problem with that, primarily since I was used to walking three consecutive days nonstop.

Again I refused to believe that I would be walking on Rwandan land, given the way everybody was describing it. The Rwanda, or the heart of it that I hoped to see, had nothing to do with forestry and dirt. It was super clean and modernized. After getting off the truck, I was still wondering if we are in Rwanda or not.

At one point, I began to really question the idea of borders, and if I had gotten out of Congo for not a thing felt different. Even the sounds of birds and the species of plants were different. Was I being duped, were we supposed to believe that this was a different country? Was I to expect that the home I had anticipated for so long was a carbon copy of the same place I had come from. Being ever the dreamer and believer, I still hoped to get to someplace lovely with a dazzling infrastructure. That was the place that I had in my imagination, but the truth was going to be something else. The people on our way popped our fantasies. We were going to live in a village where there were no roads, no electricity, nor any water taps. We were to go for miles in order to fetch a resource so primary as water. By no means am I saying that I was used to living in pleasant places, you readers are witness to it. But the days that we spent in Goma city had given me a picture of what life is like outside the forest. That had fueled my imagination, and I was expecting the same things elsewhere.

No, not just elsewhere, at home. I was expecting Rwanda to be better than anything and everything I have seen before. A land out of the books, a place where my mother grew up, where my parents met, and where education was esteemed highly. And then it was simply my home, the real one. Maybe I had too many somewhat unrealistic expectations.

But what can you expect from a child?

We walked for two hours through every inch of forestry plantation that I had expected to find on my way. We finally arrived at my mom's aunt's house. Given there was no means for communication, they had no way of expecting us.

And after decades, when they saw our family at their doorstep, they felt a miracle was transpiring before their eyes. The last time they had seen my mom was when she was getting married. What youth she must have had, how different everybody's expressions. Now, she, once a high school teacher, had resurfaced looking like a lost animal with four hungry cubs alongside here and no husband; it was no surprise that there was a lot to talk about. A lot of catching up to do.

Ten minutes after we had arrived, the whole village got gathered there, watching us as if we were some species, unlike them. The look on everyone's face screamed pity and shock and curiosity and thousand other shades of human expression. But most of all, everybody felt terribly for us, and even from among us, especially for my mom. I can't imagine relating what and how she was feeling.

She had an overwhelmed look on her face as everybody surrounding her created a rucking but flooding her with questions, interrogating like the long-lost member she was. In spite of the sadness, there was a happy quality about the people. Even when they were sad, they were anxious for us, as a sign of solidarity and empathy. When they came to express their joy, it came out through hugs, touching our faces, squeezing our cheeks and statements such as from my aunt, who said, *"She looks just like her daddy!"* During that phase of sentiment, I looked at my mom to find her overwhelm lessened. She seemed relieved to get the warm reception. They realized they should not crush her with questions, and so made her feel at home. My mom's aunts later expressed that they thought that my mom had died after they could not find any traces of her. They had given up, and so, when we suddenly arrived back on that day, that's why it seemed like a miracle was passing when they saw us.

What they did not know, though, was that my daddy passed away. We were, of course, going to tell them that at a less hectic time. They sat us down and gave us banana juice to drink, which was a surprising refreshment. I learned that it was a common drink in most villages in Rwanda. It was another first for me, tasting juice, or should I say a fruit juice for the first time in my life, and I absolutely loved it.

What I did not love, however, was the crowd and everyone on top of us. I wanted somebody to take me away because I was lost, and being the center of attention was making me more uncomfortable. After the tedious journey,

I was also tired. I wanted to sleep or at least to be left alone. But fate did not have that plan. One after another, someone would come to visit us and inquire about us from scratch. Two hours after we had arrived, my first cousin named Alia came to see us. She was so thrilled to see us that she was jumping up and down. I was exhausted, but she was the first person who made me catch her spirit, and no sooner, I too felt very excited to see her.

Amongst all the instructions she had given us, one of them was telling us about Alia. I couldn't wait to hug her after I learned about her, and now that she was before me, I didn't want to part from her. She looked much younger than mom's descriptions, which made me feel a little more comfortable. She hugged all of us siblings so tight and asked us how we were doing with authenticity and genuineness.

Unlike others, she talked directly to me instead of merely staring, which made me feel welcomed. I remember to date how good the vibes that I got from her were. It became my instant desire to befriend her, given how easily we connected. She made all my exhaustion fly away. And as fate had it, Alia became my friend from that day onwards. Even though she was older and more mature than me, I sometimes used to think that we had the same age. Life suddenly seemed more pleasant, as if living on a higher plane ever since I had a friend. I adjusted into the village life with Alia by my side. One aspect of getting into the groove was adjusting to the language. People were trying to talk to us to ascertain that we speak Kinyarwanda, and I didn't know that I had an accent. I was very fluent in Kinyarwanda, but I had a stronger Congolese accent. The difference between Rwandan and Congolese accents is the difference in the 'R' and 'L' sounds.

I most of the time pronounced them in a Congolese dialect, which seemed to amuse everyone. They not only were amused by my accent, but it also became a source of entertainment for them. It, however, led them to stare at me even more – which is something I can never grow to like.

Amidst all this hubbub, I sometimes felt like I did not belong there. It would depress me if a five-year-old can feel depressed, and I just wanted to escape; but where would I flee to? All my life had seemed to be a destiny that led me here, a land so different from the world I had formed in my head. This was not only supposed to be my home, but it was also going to be my home, which meant no more temporary residences. I had to get comfortable in my uncomfortableness. My mom was very busy catching up with her aunties and uncles, so she could not give much attention to me either. They had so many things to catch up on, including them letting my mom know that six of her siblings and her both parents had already passed away. Whether fortunately or unfortunately, my mom had heard and seen the ugly and the worst. Consequently, the news got no reaction out of her. Then again, she was very good at masking her emotions, especially in front of her kids, us. As these scenes were passing before my eyes and thoughts spinning in my mind, I realized something anew. My mom is the strongest woman I had ever seen – this fact has not changed to date.

I have seen her struggling to keep us moving alone in the DRC forests, seen her teaching us about the sky and predicting stars and weather, watched her ever be prepared for the worst, seen her in her battle-ready stance to put herself before us at any sign of danger. But then she also got her strength from us. She knew we admired her, and she knew she inspired us. It made her fearlessness grow. Simply because we all looked up to her, she wanted more than ever to be even stronger a hero for us. She had always gone the extra mile to keep us safe and borne the death of my father and her pregnancy alone. So I knew she was also going to handle that heartbreaking news about her family too. At that moment, I also discovered that I might not have that many aunties and uncles left. Do you know what that meant? It meant lesser people in the world who could have potentially been like my mom.

Even though I know as firmly as I know, there is a God that there is no one like her. It was still very tragic to hear that we had more aunts and uncles who are no more. For all its sadness, it made us feel thankful that we, our family at least, was alive anyway. One night in Rwanda, I was now trying to adjust to the fact that what I imagined were fantasies and fairytales that will never be true.

I was trying to understand that I'm going to live in the village and be a village girl, very different from the modern city girl I had in my mind. Amidst all that, I would still look up at the sky and be thankful that I now have food, shelter, security, and peace. There were no Congolese looking to hunt us, no wild animals to be fearful of, and a community to take care of us, which was to become like an extended family.

Yes, I had so much to be thankful for. I still never felt like I was at home. That unconscious yearning for a perfect place to call home still yawned here and there.

But in the life ahead to come, I discovered magnificent realities of life. I had not known that you are not handed down a home. I did not know that *"You create your own home – it is what you make upon your soil."*

But I was going to.

New Home

Our family was looking good at settling in the warm and boisterous village of Vunga. It had a different air from our settlements in Congo; most prominent among them was the home and community feels. Over here, my mom was trying to find us a place to stay and move out of her aunt's house. It was like a small cottage, which was small for all of us. We were never used to living with a big family and being dependent on someone else.

Add to that, the suffocation it all brought. I don't know who it was, but someone suggested that we go over to check mom's parents' house. But we didn't go with her. Mom suggested we stay back at her cousin's place. She went with her friends there who helped my mother clean it so that we could move in.

They told us that it took great labor and effort, and you could tell, given that it took them three days' worth of cleaning. But all of them told us the final result was satisfactory. When it was ready for our presentation, we went over to check it. The house was isolated from all the other houses. I loved that it was built on a mountain, which was an exhilarating prospect. Our nearest neighbors were one whole mile away from home. It was like a castle, and you could tell from the outside how spacious it would be on the inside. Touring the place, we found our voices echo in the enormous rooms. From the window we could see a yard too, which meant fun and games for us. Everything was old, but one could tell that it once must have been the best house in the village before it got withered with time.

My mom's friends and aunties gave us some of the basic needs, such as cooking pans, plates, forks, and spoons. It was a minimalistic place at the start of those days. We didn't have a lot of things in the house, but it was good to have a place that I call home – not just nation-wise but residentially too. Again, it was not my ideal home, but it was *"our place."* I wasn't going to be ungrateful about that, not even at the age of five.

Our status as a celebrity hadn't declined even after a week. We would have visitors arriving every day to check on us. Along with their 'How are you doing', they will bring for us food such as green beans, bananas, yams, and cassava that would go on to last for like a week. Everyone in the village was a farmer. Not surprisingly, we were living among subsistence farmers who produced small for home consumption. They ate what they cultivated, and whatever access they would acquire, they would share with the other members of the community. That's why every visitor brought us some of their produce. After that, we were going to take care of our groceries. We also had our share of rice and oil from the Nkamira transit center, and my mom will cook us rice once per week. It was our mutually favorite meal.

Neither in the village nor at home was there anything interesting to do. Every day was a replica copy of the previous one. I had nothing to do other than regular house chores. Some change would come when my mom would take us to visit her friends and her other extended family members that we didn't know about. During that eventfulness was life would seem pretty decent.

Add to that that I made a few friends more friends other than Alia pretty quickly. As you have already seen, the kids in the village were very welcoming to us, and they held us to a reverential height. We were outsiders to them, and that brought a sense of exoticism. You could see it in their giggling eyes that our strange accent was special for them. Every time I would go to fetch water at the community water tap, I'd both meet several people who would cheerfully regard and indulge me, and also find those whom I would hear whisper *"that's Jeanne's daughter."* Other people would call my name, wave, or ask me how I'm doing. That formality and camaraderie were part of the community life in Rwanda. You may be acquainted with many people, but only a few of them knew who you were. As far as I go, I was a stranger kid with a Congolese accent. And that's it.

I remember I used to watch kids in school uniforms and wished I was one of them. I wanted to go to school so badly. The desire made a patient person like me grow impatient. To address your confusion, the reason why we were not enrolled in school was that the semester was almost ending. We couldn't start school right away and had to get admission after it ended.

I had two outfits when I came to Vunga village, but thanks to my cousin and friend Alia, I had a dozen or so more. She was older and more significant than me, so her outgrown clothes came to my jolly good use. I had so many of them that I would share some with my sister. That did not erase the fact that we were poor kids from an impoverished family.

That was reinforced all the more when a few weeks later, my mom sold one of her family lands. She needed the money, and no opportunity was knocking on the door. Her wealthy parents had passed away without leaving anything but land, so that was all the monetary support we had for the time being. I'm not sure how much money she got, but what I know is that she took us shopping from it. I feel the need to fulfill my future children's desires. I understand how dissatisfying it feels to have your child writhing with yearnings and you not having anything to please them.

Out shopping, it was my first time being at a large crowded market. It felt so pleasant to be amidst such beautiful stuff, and I loved trying on different clothes even if we were not going to buy all of them. We did buy some new pairs of clothes – in fact, too many clothes now that I think in retrospect – and then shoes as well. I have always wanted to own shoes, even if it made my feet feel awkward and unfamiliar. So it was a minor dream come true.

Post-shopping, I had two pairs of shoes. One to take to church and one for everyday use. My mom did some grocery shopping as well, whereby she bought some potatoes, more rice, cooking oil, and beans. I instantly felt like we had become wealthy. I simultaneously knew my mother was not silly enough to spend all the money on shopping. How could she not have saved for the rainy days? Staring at my two pairs of shoes, I had a hard time believing they were mine. I would be so hesitant to wear my shoes on a dirt floor. I wanted to keep them like how a child keeps a brand new iPhone today, clean and safe all the time. But of course, that was not possible around the mud that surrounded our house and was a feature of the whole village.

I practiced how to walk in my new shoes every single day. It was an act that had to be mastered, like skating shoes, or like walking in high heels for the first time. It may come as a dismay to you that my 'shoes' were, in fact, slippers. I could now clean my feet and keep them clean in my new 'shoes.'

It was an alien concept I was familiarizing with; something that had never happened before. Life was, in many ways, becoming better and better every day. Yet, no matter how much I tried to feel like I belonged in that village, the feeling just never felt right. It was more like trying to convince myself than actually feeling it. I knew deep down that I don't like living in the village even though that's the life I had been exposed to ever since I was born. But I still didn't feel like I belong there. It always felt temporary and hollow on the inside like those rubber balls we used to play with. I had not known that it was more like a transition phase for me. I was by no means the only one who was feeling like that. My mom related to me. She was a city girl who was born and raised in the village. As part of a default heritage, I felt like I belonged to the city too. Then something auspicious happened.

We had an aunt, my mother's younger sister, named Mary. She lived in the city. Aunt Mary heard about our return and planned to come to visit us. Now, before I go on, something about Aunt Mary's personality. She is an easy-going stress-free person who loves living in the moment and having fun. She was that impulsive kind who did what her heart told her.

Aunt Mary hated village life, and she, fortunately, married someone who lived in Kigali city. They were a middle-class family with three kids. These were all the things I had heard about her. When I saw her, the first thing I noticed was that she looked exactly like my mom. She brought us sweet bread and several good quality city clothes and shoes. Not only for us, but she also brought clothes for my mom too. I was immediately infatuated with her. Listening to her elicited joy and thrill in me and made me so badly want to go with her to the city.

But my mom had other plans.

She wanted my older sister to go with Mary so that she can find her a private tutor for two months of homeschooling. My sister was too old to start school in the same class as me, so my mom thought that if they can find her a tutor over the summer, she will be able to skip two elementary school years (primary one and primary two) and go directly to primary three.

It sounded like a perfect idea, although I didn't know how my sister was going to manage it. My mom was protecting her from feeling bad about being the oldest kid in her class. So once again, she went into her instruction mode and reassured her in the best way possible. It was heartwarming to see. She wanted all of us to have a regular and good education like everybody else, regardless of our unique situation.

And as for me being left behind, I did not feel so bad about it. The most dominant sensation I felt for the next months was missing my sister. I myself did not know that I would, but I did. The worst part was that there was no medium of communication between us. I mean other than the hope in my heart that she is doing fine. I wanted to see her, be with her.

I couldn't wait to hear all about Kigali and how much fun she had. I wanted to know about the city experience, about the food she ate, the friends she made and the new clothes they bought her. Those were my fantasies at the time. As for what was going on back in the village, my mom bought me a school uniform, and I was looking forward to starting school in two months.

My mom also tried finding a job since she was a teacher and still had her high school diploma. That was the only thing we could place our hopes on for a steady income. Much thanks to God, it didn't take that long for her to find a teaching position at the nearest primary (elementary) school. Auspiciously, it would turn out to be the same school that my sister and I would be going to study at. Three weeks into our new house, a person who had long been absent from our life (and from this book, too) came to visit us: John. I'm not sure how he heard about our news, so my initial impressions were he has some secret spies. He always somehow learns about us. But my fantasy bubbles burst when I, later on, learned that he and my mom used to write letters to each other. John had been in Rwanda for a month before we arrived.

He had also found an excellent job, given that he was also educated. His entry shocked everyone at our place, primarily because he had been gone for so long, and it was such a pleasant surprise. And then secondly, he looked so dashing. He appeared to be the personification of a thriving self-made man. The instant my mom saw him, it was as if the wilted flower in her heart that she had been hiding from us, bloomed again.

John also beamed so wide that there was no mistaking the amount of love and aching between the two. As for me, I was not over the fact that my mom replaced my daddy. I couldn't quite explain back then why I felt that way for so long, but I can reason now. I loved my daddy so much, and he passed away and was replaced too soon. He died at the time my family needed him the most. It was God's plan; I cannot question it, but that doesn't change how deep a heartache that instilled in me. As for John, he was a nice person and he both loved and cared for us so much, just like his children; like he will bring us new city food such as bread, candies and juices and clothes to wear. Plus, he was smart too. He seemed genuinely in love with my mom, and I liked that about him. She also felt happy in his company, not just that masked happy but happy from deep, deep in her soul. In the end, the balance was looking to tip towards the good that John was for us.

He was officially our step-dad, and I couldn't deny that. I just had to adjust to it, and I knew that I needed to. There was every reason to. He would spend many days at home, helping my mom with farming and planting crops. He would also sometimes disappear to someplace all of a sudden, and I initially did not understand that.

I, later on, I learned that he had a job somewhere else, and that's where he would go to. Here was a man who was becoming a backbone of our family, and still looking after his responsibilities too. How could I not appreciate and accept him? I had to find a way to preserve respect and adoration for my father, while maintaining a relationship with my step-father, too. Times were finally showing activity and pleasantness. My life was changing every day. I was about to start school, and I had a working step daddy and a mother who was soon becoming a teacher with a salary. I could not hold back saying back then that life was good. More good news: My sister finally came back. Her skin looked lighter and smoother than it was when she left. I suspected it might have been because of some quality skin lotion, clean water, and good food – all the essentials of urban lifestyle.

I shouldn't shy away from also saying that she looked gorgeous, too. I had to hold myself back from letting my jaw fall. I couldn't believe it was my sister that I was looking at. Two months mere and her Congolese accent had faded from compared to when we were together. She looked perfect to me.

After her return and settling everything down, we spent the whole night talking together. I can't tell you that, but throughout that time, I was exploding with curiosity to learn about the city and all her experiences. She told me about my aunt, who, despite her sophistication, sometimes would get crazy and scream at everyone at home. She also mentioned that they had two housemaids who were taking care of everything in the modern-styled house of the likes we had never seen. My sister's days consisted of nothing other than studying. She told me all about our cousins too. They sounded somewhat like arrogant people in general, but gratefully, they treated her with kindness and good manners. She described one of my cousins named Eva (my aunt's firstborn), as tall, very beautiful with long, relaxed straight hair.

Eva knew and spoke fluent French with her mom and daddy at home. All her friends communicated in French, which to my sister was a lyrical and sweet-sounding tongue. In my mind, all of these things sounded unreal. I felt the curiosity I felt prior to talking about it with my sister had inflated all the more. I couldn't wait to meet the elegant Eva, though I didn't know when and how. I

couldn't wait to breathe the city air and experience the malls, the schools, even the traffics and roads. I wanted to absorb every little thing. My sister described road lights in Kigali to me, and how the cars have to stop when it turns red and move when it turns green. I listened to it with so much awe, because this felt like out of a movie to me. I had countless questions, like who controls the lights, who turns them on and off, and from where the green and red color come? Unfortunately, my sister had no answers to my questions. But I was okay with that. I wanted to discover it on my own.

My Education Journey

It was January of 2003 when I first put my foot in school. I was too old for nursery classes, so I went straight to elementary school – which in my country we call primary school. I was six years old at that time, though I looked like a four years old girl. I was thrilled about the school, for you know it had been my dream to be enrolled in one. I wanted to be educated too, like my mom, my daddy, my stepdaddy.

My mom had bought me large-sized uniforms so that I would eventually grow into them. This way, she would not have to spend on them again. As it turned out, my tiny body was pretty lost in the school uniform. I was as a person in a bunny costume; you could hardly see me. Our female uniform included blue long skirts and t-shirts, and khaki uniforms for boys.

That was a common uniform for all the public schools in Rwanda. I would carry two notebooks in my hands, one for all the classwork of courses and another one for school homework. You can say that I was as ready for school as one could be. By extension, I was prepared for my future – the future which I could mold as per my desire and ambitions; my efforts, my dedication was the secret ingredient to this recipe. It did not depend upon my birthplace. With education, I could thrive and sour and give myself the life that I always wanted and maybe make for myself the 'home' as it was in my imagination. I could fulfill my desire to settle in and flourishing in city life. Perhaps I would have called my mother too. I was brimming with excitement, and the beginning of my schooling journey spurred all of it. As I told you, my mom was a teacher at the same school my sister and I was studying at. She introduced me to almost every school teacher at my school.

It established my reputation as Jeanne's daughter, so that everybody, teachers, and students included, knew that my mother was the teacher. I was cool with it at that time. I was, after all, getting the kids' respect for that reason. I was more important than an average student in my class, and this was before the classes had even started.

The first day went by too fast. It was like an enjoyable amusement ride that is over too soon. That said, I loved everything about school right away. I was eager to learn, and I was eager for the next day. The only thing I hated was that everybody got hooked by my accent. I was an object of amazement and amusement. It made me more of an immediate center of attention as the teacher's daughter. They could tell that I wasn't from the area and I hated it. To my surprise, I wasn't the only one who had a mother as her teacher. My seatmate, named Alain, was another teacher's son. We seemed to get along so well, and both knew that each secretly liked the other. Alain would stare at me whenever I was looking away, and I would make sure that he doesn't see that I'm aware of him staring at me.

And then I would do the same: look at him when his attention was elsewhere. Only God knows if he knew I was looking at him and pretended the same way I did. We avoided making eye contact as much as we could. In fact, such was our shyness that I don't remember us ever having one. Alain was a cute and memorable part of the school journey.

Despite skipping nursery school, I can still say that school was an exceptional experience. I earned the rank as the topper of my class for the first semester. They used to announce the top student's name in every class, and the time came at the end of the semester, my mom was so delighted with me. She had a look of pride on her face when they called my name. That was it, and I just knew that I did well. For the first time in my life, I was witnessing something that made my mom very proud of me: my grades. My sister, who had skipped two school years, was doing great as well. My mom was guiding her and helping her out a lot during the afterschool hours. At home, my mom would tell us that she doesn't have any treasure or any money or possessions to give us. *"If there is one thing I can offer you,"* she would tell us, *"that's education."* She told us that the only way to reach a successful place in life is through education.

She would emphasize this a lot. Sometimes, in order to motivate us, she would remind us of how intelligent my dad was. He was among the smartest students in the country, according to his academic records, and that was among the reasons why mom married him. I, to this date, feel very lucky that I have smart parents. It ensured that we were also bright as it passed down to us genetically, too.

Everybody who knew our parents' academic background held us reverentially. It would sometimes feel like a lot of pressure and expectations were on us. But we almost always delivered on it. One day, I'm living my first day of school classes; the next day, I'm watching my first school year go by. It was that fast. Once again, I was the top student in my class. All of my teachers loved me for it and saw great potential in me. They would say so themselves. From that time onwards, being the top student in my classes became my goal. My mom's words of how education is the only thing she had to offer were a constant reminder that I have to excel academically. Despite me being very young, I knew I wanted to give my mom the best life that my dad was not able to provide, both to her and ourselves. My personal goal was to make my mom happy and to be rich, just so that I could buy her whatever my daddy would have bought her.

I knew that education was my weapon in that regard. It was the ultimate tool that would carve my worth. By fulfilling and delivering on that responsibility, I secretly hoped to accomplish my daddy's responsibilities of being there for my family. I wanted to step into my daddy's shoes and be another version of him in my family. I aspired to pick up where he left off.

Till when was my mom supposed to struggle for our progress? I wanted to grow independent. I know it is too much for seven-year-olds to be thinking about, but these stresses went about in my mind. It pained me to watch that woman almost give up her life for us. My dad, when he was alive, did the same too. So, I surely had a mission to do something more significant in my life. And that big thing was going to make me become my family's support and a source of their ease and peace. This was going to be my top priority; this was going to be my life purpose. Knowing what I wanted in life at the age of seven pushed me to be more focused than others. I was filled with determination as a student. My routine and lifestyle were much different from other kids my age.

I wouldn't spend much time in the playground, and my lunch breaks would be shorter. I would go home straight after school, I would bury myself in my homework, revising what I learned at school. It was my everyday goal to satisfy my mother and make her proud. After the first school year, my stepdad proposed to us that we shift our village to where he worked and stay with him.

He would usually come home to visit us over the weekend. Since he lived in a good place with better schools, he would pitch the idea casually. He wanted me and my sister to come live with him. But gradually, his wish grew more ardent, and we started entertaining it after my first school year. On the holiday of December 2003, we moved to my step-father's city called Gisenyi. It was next to

Rwanda and DR Congo border. Given the reputation my step-father had established, I was excited for here. I bred expectations, and it delivered on them. It was surprising because our passage to the city was not well-developed nor impressive. We thought we were moving back to refugee camps in DR Congo. It was all jungle and heaths and wilderness and dust.

We children started crying because we didn't want to go back again. True, our village wasn't the place I had dreamed of, but it was still better than living on our own in the wild. My mom assured us that we are not moving back. It indeed was a relief. Gisenyi was beautiful and civilized than where we had come from. The first thing you lay your eyes on is greenery, as well as the last.

The streets I found to be mostly unpaved, but even in that, they were better. Our new home was way big a jump and upgrade from where we lived before, too. It was close to the main road with a developed infrastructure. There was electricity everywhere, planted along the roadsides. Water taps gave every house easy access to water. My life over there began changing very quickly. I kind of felt like we had become a little wealthier, which was true. Thanks to my step-father. I have always loved living in the city, and my mom loved it as well. My initial dream of the home I wanted was slowly morphing to be the city of Gisenyi. It was getting me closer to where I wanted to live. I did later learn that it was not the best city in Rwanda, but it was better than any village with no electricity or clean water – which was every place we had thus far lived at. I chuckle now, thinking that I had suspected it would be like that refugee camp.

My mom began trying to transfer schools there right away, both for herself and me. No sooner, I got an admission in a new school there. As usual, and much thanks to God, I was the leading student in all of my classes. Nobody else's track was better than mine, not for one month. I became the top student for the whole academic year, and that was the source of pride and delight for my mom.

I loved that. Her happiness gave me a greater push to remain pursuing excellence. My family and I were now all getting used to my academic excellence. I should be honest, not only was my mother content with my performance as a student, I was too. I loved being an exceptional student. Being hungry for knowledge. Being one of those who loved school so much that they never missed days and loved getting up early and preparing gladdened me. And then, from a younger age, when we weren't really compelled, I would still take out time at home to revise whatever I studied. It was very unusual for other students in my class to hear. Equally, it was odd for me to hear they did not practice similarly. My mom never had to remind me what to do when it came to schoolwork. It was all possible, and I had internalized what education meant for my future.

I was empathetic about my family's struggles. But after my realization and efforts put, things were looking good. And then a few months after we had moved to our new place, my mom got pregnant. But it would be unfair to put it that way. She was, in fact, pregnant before we had moved in. In retrospect, that possibly could have been one of the reasons why we moved here.

You understand, right? Being a middle-aged woman with four children already, she didn't want to be judged by village people. They already thought that she moved on too fast. Then add to that she was with another husband and was expecting a child with him. If you ask me, I personally wished she didn't have to give birth again. But as you can feel, I was starting to grow more and more of a tender spot for my mother. She deserved the happiness that was snatched from her too. Also, since her new husband had no kids, it made sense to have a child, especially as they both seemed to be in love. I now also don't like the idea that my stepfather was supporting our entire family without having a child of his own blood. Unfortunately, the closer and closer baby number five was to its arrival, the lesser and lesser I liked the situation. I was aware that the new kid is a little different from us since we had different dads.

But then I had conflicting thoughts saying it did not matter anyway. We were all from the same mother, after all. That's all mattered to me, I would tell myself. At first, I didn't know how to act when the newborn finally came. My stepdad had been more than prepared for him, and I remember yearning for this kind of love. I had never experienced it in my life from my father, because of the scarcity of experiences I had with him.

Interesting fact, all of my brothers were born after I was born in bushes. Do you know what that means? That means they were born in the worst conditions you can ever think of. And then they barely had clothes to wear. In this way too, John's childhood was different from us all. I felt like John was doing the most and probably a little extra preparing for his firstborn. But as you can tell, I was just jealous of the love I never received. Perhaps, if I was born in the same conditions, they could have made a big deal out of that too. We named my third brother Sena. It was a special day for my family, especially my stepdad, who seemed very excited. The grin on his face was so wide. I didn't remember my father being as happy for either of my brothers.

But one thing was commendable about John. He loved Sena the same way he loved us. I admit the shortcoming that I was still not too comfortable with John. Not half as much as I would be to my own daddy. But on his part, he tried to be an excellent dad. Every Christmas, my mother, and John would spend New Year's Eve with John's family. They lived far away from where we stayed in the most rural place I have ever seen.

Coming from me, you know what that means that it was way worse than where we used to live. They would take Sena with them as well since my sister and I had never been interested in going there. My mom didn't seem to like it much. I remember her sighs and drearily packing things up as we prepared to head to her in-laws. But she had to do it.

It was her new family now, after all. Every time she would return home, my mom would be infused with stories. Peasant appearances, cow dung, windows as frail as palm leaves; she despised that lifestyle, but I suppose she was more scarred due to her past. Now that we had been living in an adequate place, which we felt like we deserved after a lifetime of struggle, we wanted to remain with it. Mom would also narrate that John was the only educated man in his family. She would describe the kind of food they eat. Not only the kind but also the way they eat. It was funnier than was insulting, though.

They would have eggs and bread on their plates, but they wouldn't eat the two together. Picking the fried egg in one hand and the bread in the other, they would munch the two separately. We would gather and listen to these oddities intently, laughing till our guts ached. I loved to hear all about them from my mom. She relayed it so passionately. It was still surprising that in spite of despising the lifestyle, my mom would visit every Christmas eve. I think it said something about how much my mom loved him. Sometimes I would also wonder if she truly loved him in that sense as much. Why would I wonder this? Because even in his company at times, she would say something nice about my passed-away dad. These would be things such as how unique an occasion their wedding was. She would also talk about my dad's smartness and his intelligence. And John's reaction? He was fine with it. He would smile at dad's mention and nod his head. I knew my mom never brought dad up because of hurting John. She missed him. But I also don't think it was only because she missed him that she did this. She probably also wanted us to never forget our dad, despite moving on. I don't think it was possible in any way to forget him. I remembered him every day and at night.

Sometimes John's sister, Kankindi, would come to visit us. When I saw her the first time, I found that she looked exactly how my mom described her; peasant, shabby, short girl, who ate like she had visitors in her stomach. My mom would cook the most delicious meals while Kankindi was there. The woman loved the food so much, and she would hardly ever get full. Kankindi seemed very indigenous, but very nice and kind also. My mom would give her extra attention every time. She wanted to maintain a good reputation with the family of John, who had a number of favors on us.

I hated the whole time she was at home, as my mom would shift her whole attention to Kankindi. It was awkward because John's relatives neither felt like my family members nor my friends. They were just polite strangers to me. My days would be spent keeping up with my studies and dedicating a portion of my time to household chores. That was my everyday life. Eventually, out of my mom's desire to give us the best and comfortable life, she found a housemaid for us.

She was worried about my older sister having back pain because of all of the physical struggles she went through. It indeed was too tender an age for her to be carrying that burden. But thanks to the maid, neither me nor she had to invest much physically around the house.

My life had been growing better and better back then eventually. My family was above the poverty line. We classified as an average income earning family with living standards that had improved drastically in a concise period. It wasn't even what they call exponential growth today. It was a spiked growth. Sudden. They usually say that life can change in the blink of an eye. My life had changed just like that, and from that point onwards, it was slowly and slowly creeping up on the charts. Despite me being the top student in all my classes, or perhaps due to that, my mom made sure I enrolled in another program. It was called 'Cours du Soir' and was designed to help students take their knowledge to the next level. We were to learn and apply things that were beyond our regular syllabus. This was to be done by repeating the class materials and solving additional exercises after school. Yes, it took place in our school, but after our regular day when school was over. They were more like evening classes. In fact, *Cours du Soir* actually means evening classes in French

I felt that it was a privilege for me to be in that program for multiple reasons. Firstly, my knowledge and learning were expanding further. I always did believe that I could gain more than I was getting out of my classes. And they say learning more, reading and discovering things help make neural pathways in your head that improve critical thinking. I was getting that.

Then secondly, you had to pay an extra amount of money to your school teacher for these classes. I had that going for me too, for my mom was paying the fee. Education was the first priority in my family. Everything else came after. Work first, play later. Thanks to *'Cours du Soir'* and my responsible mother, I was by then growing super smarter in classes. I felt like I was growing to know everything about the world and my country. When I arrived during the following summer holidays, my mom urged us to work, either part-time or full. *"You should find ways to make money so that you could afford to buy your own school materials and clothes,"* she said. She not only wanted us to excel in school, but she also wanted to train us to be financially responsible and independent. She gave my sister and me eight hundred Rwandan francs (800 RWF), which is approximately one U.S dollar today. This was our capital. I had an idea where we could invest it in.

I had seen kids selling sugarcane by the roadsides. Little stalls with a machine installed. There were vendors too who would feed several canes, about eight to twelve at a time, into the mouth of a machine and out would pour the rich, thick creamy green juice with a natural foam on the top. But we weren't looking to go that grand. Not already. Perhaps someday we could have. But for now, the former idea was pleasant, selling plain sugarcanes by the roadside. I thought we could do that, especially since it was very cheap. Our capital would suffice in order to help us start. And so, we went ahead and bought five long sugar cane sticks and began selling them at a busy footpath. What was hard about that business was that the place where we used to acquire our sugarcanes (at the lower price) was very far. We had to travel all the way to a sugar cane plantation. It was three hours away from my home, but we did it anyway.

Our summer livelihood depended on it. And then it wasn't the first time we were contributing to our family. Every member, since childhood, worked in some way and procured something to bring to the table, for example, by hunting. I was born struggling, and so that did not seem to be a big deal to me.

Selling sugar cane went well for the most part. We sometimes made a profit, rarer times a hefty profit too. What started as five sugarcanes would go to fifty. However, what I hated most about the business was that I had to hide from students at school. It was embarrassing to see a teacher's daughter selling sugar cane at the roadside. I couldn't have been caught doing that. It was something that only a school dropout used to do. And then I was too young to be doing business. If it wasn't for this, I would have been proud of myself. I perhaps was… maybe. There was nothing like being young in my family when you were treated like a responsible adult. I understood and liked that. But I would still feel embarrassed most of the time whenever, for instance, one of my teachers passed by. Sometimes it would be a student, sometimes a staff member. Or any other person that I knew. The smile on my face would instantly fade, and I would try to hide as much as I could.

That was until I finally gave up. I was primarily worried about being bullied at school and possibly given nicknames because of selling sugar cane sticks, a job for school dropout. But then I accepted it eventually for what it was. I owned it with an attitude that comes with it. It was only two months, after all.

Fortunately, no one tried to nickname me. The business went so well that by the end of the summer holiday, we both made three more dollars as profit. We returned the initial investment to my mother, and each one of us took a dollar. It was an occasion to celebrate. I truly felt rich, on my own grounds, for the first time in my life. One dollar was priceless at the time for me. It could buy me five notebooks, two pens, chewing gums, and maybe a donut as well. Guess what I used my money for? I used my money to buy a few notebooks. With the rest, I bought second-hand clothes! At one time, one of the things that I had been deprived of was clothes. But by now, I had grown to love clothes so much. Time and again, I would go to the market and look for second-hand clothes that cost a few cents. I was over the moon when I was able to buy one skirt and one dress. It was the day that I not only bought my first clothes from my own money but also when I started shopping for my own clothes. And by that, I mean till today.

After some weeks, we moved to a different house. It happened to be closer to my school. Prior to moving, my sister and I used to walk for one hour every day to get to school. And then another hour it would take to return. It seemed nothing to me, to us since I, since we, had walked way farther than this during our most difficult days. I wouldn't lie, I actually enjoyed the morning walks on my way to school. We just had to be careful of the cars on the roads – yes, there were many cars in this town. We had a group of students whom we lived in the same neighborhood. Together we would leave our house around 6:45 AM so that we could reach before 8 AM.

The new place we moved to was closer to my school. In this neighborhood, I met the girl who would grow to become my first best-friend. Her name was Rose. She was the coolest kid around and the more affluent kid in the entire village. That wasn't why I befriended her, of course. We just clicked the very first day I saw her. It was an automatic connection.

Her family was way richer than anybody else's I have ever seen. They lived in a mansion, all royal and classic at the same time. They had a luxurious German car whose name I forgot. A white woman lived with them. Inside their home, they would speak French, and I would just watch her mouth dribble out the words sensually. She carried the rich kid look effortlessly with her clear and smooth skin and everything shipshape.

On the other hand, I was like an average kid who would be more acutely aware of her averageness in Rose's company. By that, I mean in terms of wealth and immaculateness. Nevertheless, I wouldn't let that scar me. I knew that I was extremely talented and very smart, and these qualities mattered to me. I was passionate and had the reputation of being cool. I would sometimes overhear people saying that my accent was even cooler. I forgot to tell you that my mom was a teacher again in this school of ours too. Every teacher grew to love me for my performance and personality. I was also very mature for my age. I would always try to remain organized, which felt like a difficult feat for others in my class. Even as an average child, I was very fashionable, since I bought my own clothes. I was physically flexible and athletic – I owe that to my childhood adventures. Along with being a diligent student, I would play jump rope games and could jump as high as two meters. I would run as fast as some bikes. Due to this, everybody wanted me on their team.

Perhaps it was these qualities that impressed Rose. Despite being average, I reckon she saw that I wasn't ordinary. And so Rose and I became friends. Rose herself was effortlessly smart, and we spent almost all the time together, except when we had to sleep in our separate houses and had to relieve ourselves, of course. Rose's mother had a shop of bridal dresses and flowers. She was a wedding planner and would also rent wedding dresses and flowers. On Valentine's Day, the concept I hadn't known about by then, Rose surprised me with a beautiful flower bouquet. Don't tell anyone, but she had stolen that from her mom's shop. It was ostentatious, with roses and carnations and chrysanthemums and flowers I do not know the names of. Following that 14th February, I started celebrating Valentine's Day with my friends. (Friends, yes). Rose was incredibly loving and very nice. She didn't have that rich people vanity or that pomposity about her. We seemed to be more than best friends at times and could do anything for one another.

Oh, I should probably mention that we didn't take classes together. Rose was one class ahead of me, and that was how that went. All of our free time in school would be spent together. Rose and I were the popular kids at school. And that status brought with it its perks. By that, I mean to say we had bodyguards, two boys who happened to be my friends and neighbors and classmates. I enjoyed that, for it made me feel like a queen.

Rose's mom was very impressed when she had learned that I was the smartest kid at school. She was genuinely interested in knowing about my family and me. And she learned. I admire that she was intrigued and respectful towards the struggles my family and I had been through. She listened to me intently with her humble grandeur and asked all questions politely at the right places. She really wanted our friendship to work and last longer. Rose's mother probably saw potential in me, and my personality intrigued her too. I was right shades of religious too, something that Rose's family abundantly was. As Catholics, her parents were immensely respected at the local catholic church. Due to that, Rose was one of the kids who served wine and bread to the priests.

It was a great privilege to, and she had a right to that. Along with that, she would also sit at the front of a five-hundred church congregation with people wearing white dresses, matching the priests'. Because of Rose, I started getting involved in the Catholic Church too. This included me going for Sunday school with my best friend. I also went ahead and joined a kids' dance group.

They used to dance during Sunday church services, and it was so pleasurable for me. My command over my body developed a greater stronghold. And so, in this manner, my schedule turned into this: school and Rose's house and church and school and Rose's house and church. One part of Rose and my friendship was sharing chewing gums. We loved them so much, and Rose always had money to buy them. Me, on the other hand, I would sometimes go for a month without getting a dime from my mom. But whenever I did, I would also buy chewing gums for both of us. With my successes at school of a bright topper, I started growing more far-sighted. I decided upon goals of which high school I would prefer to go to after my elementary school. That is always a hectic part of choosing because now you are propelling towards your future.

Out of the many options, you have to select one. One. I know it is more difficult for universities, but that time was to come for me too eventually. I had heard people talk about Catholic schools too. Especially all-women schools had a good reputation in my country. Only the cream of the crop, both in regards to teachers and students, make it over there. And thus, making it there became another of my goals.

This is what I would do. I would set my goals and then would compete with myself in every possible manner to finally reach them. This worked best for academics. At that time, my goal was to do well in the national exams so that I could get admission into the best all-women Catholic schools. I prayed every day for that. National exams were the only exams that determined if you are going for high school or not. They also decided that if you are going, which high school are you going to. The equation was simple: the higher the grades, the better the high school. My school teachers, aunties, and uncles all had so much faith in me. They knew I would do well in the national exams. I had faith in me too, but this pressure was not good for me. I would grow worried about disappointing everyone.

But then it benefitted also, for I studied even harder to make all of them proud of me. I had a reputation to maintain in the eyes of my class, as well as my own eyes. And my reputation was of being the smartest kid at school. Sometimes, my mom thought I was over-studying because none of my other classmates were studying. She would watch them outdoors, playing, and casually going about their lives.

But I had a goal in my heart, and I was determined to achieve it. Yes, I was different, and I admitted it. I was different in ways that I think and did things. But it was all about my family and me. I wanted to pick up where my dad left off, and that could only be done if I do well in school and become educated and successful. Furthermore, I had a personal goal of being independent and creating a place that

I wanted to call home. So what if it didn't exist exactly as I conceived? So what if Rwanda was a disappointment on the surface level. It still had the potential, and what I created was up to me. I had not yet found a home, and I was determined to make one. The same fancy place I had in my imagination, I wanted to build it for myself and my people. I wanted to make that healthy life for myself. I knew it would require sacrifices, but I was head-on prepared for that.

Sometimes, at home, we would have arguments about the way things happen in life. Others would express frustration and ill-humor, but I always seemed to have a different opinion from the rest. It took my mom a while to get used to me having different opinions all the time. The Misfits aren't easy to comply with, after all. In Rwandan culture, kids, especially women, do not raise their voices fueled with their opinions so much.

They mostly don't even feel the need to. Our culture expected women to stay silent, passively accept the treatment given to them. But no, I wasn't one of those women and was neither going to be. I was very young but very opinionated. It didn't matter who I was talking to or how old one looked. I was about the truth. If I don't agree with what you had said, I will point out my opinion. If you said something that felt right to me and it was an unpopular opinion, I would make sure to appreciate it regardless of others. Sometimes my mom would point out that I was disrespectful by arguing with people who are older than me. Sure, that may be how it appeared to them, but I didn't care. That wasn't my truth. My thing was honest. That was me, and I wasn't harming anyone with the character I had. Whatever they thought I was, it was their problem. They had to deal with it.

This was why I sometimes did not click with my sister. She was the opposite. My sister, just like any other kid, was very modest and shy even when she didn't agree with what you would be saying. She will still act as if she agrees with you. This quality made it easy for her to fit in and live in peace with everyone. Something that wasn't my priority.

I remember once in a while, my sister and I would go to visit my aunties who lived in different cities. As always, my mom had to give us instructions on what we should and should not do. She told us that we represent her in every house we entered, and she needed to be represented as a good parent.

That was the pressure on our shoulders. But no doubt, the point was valid. She told us that we need to wake up early in the morning before my cousins and help their housemaids. She mentioned that we should eat very respectfully, without talking while chewing our food. She guided us to leave the last piece of food for young kids. She also had to mention to me that I should not try to argue with anyone. This was something she said with her eyes wide at me, and very slowly but surely.

She asked me to do whatever my aunt said. And did things go precisely as my mom had expected? Nope. I didn't wake up before my cousins to do their house chores? Why was that rude of me? No, because they had two housemaids of their own. My mom knew that, and yet she was insisting on it. I was instructed to do things I don't do even at my home.

However, I was supposed for the sake of my mom's reputation. After all, we were visitors. I mean, if a guest came to my house and they had a paid housemaid, I wouldn't have had them do their dishes and make their bed and sweep the floors. I was the same age as my cousin and thought it was not fair for my sister and I to do all their house chores.

You can guess what my sister would have done. You can also imagine what I would have done. Or rather, wouldn't have done. My sister carried out the chores, precisely as my mom had instructed. I mean, I tried to help, but then I got tired and stopped. I felt like a maid more than a guest. It didn't make that much sense to me. I would see my sister struggling to please my aunt and found it immoral.

She worked more than their housemaids. She too, like me, didn't want to do it, but for my mom's sake, she did the work. As usual, whenever I didn't agree with something, I had the confidence and courage always to raise my voice and call out. I did just that, and as a result, my aunt thought I was arrogant.

In fact, everyone except my mom felt that I was a prickly, arrogant kid. This included the way I dress right up to my opinions. I was very different from an 'ideal' Rwandan kid. I have told my mom on several occasions that I can't pretend to be someone else just because we are not at home. I needed to be always myself, for better or worse. Growing up feeling different in my family made me feel like something was wrong with me at times. Sometimes I would beat myself to keep quiet and keep my opinions to myself. Yet, I failed on many occasions. I started feeling like my mom doesn't like me as much as she was fond of my sister. Whether she understood me or not was unimportant. Every relative praised my sister on how nice she was, and how respectful she was. They would tell my mom that she did an impeccable job of raising my sister. All because she does all their house chores whenever she visits them. I knew my sister didn't like it, but she would rather be praised than being hated for being herself.

Listening to all that validation, I sometimes wished I was like my sister. I wished I would behave like her, and I wished I could silence the little voice in me that makes me different from the rest. As it so happened, the people started making me detest that stubborn noisy voice inside me. So many inner conflicts later, I realized that nope, it was inevitable. It was me. That's who I was.

As if these differences weren't enough, my differences were also very prominent in my fashion styles as well. I hated long skirts and loose clothes. I hated the mainstream and the typically feminine items. I hated the outfit that every kid in the village had or liked, and thus, I wanted something unique. Something that would make me stand out. Before I had started buying my own clothes, I was always complaining about clothes that my mom would buy for me. I liked shopping for myself. It was more of my thing. I would buy a conventional skirt design and take it to the tailors so that they can modify it and make it a little more unique. I would embroider it with my creativity. I would have it stitched as per my imagination.

When people saw my clothes, they would all wonder where I shopped. They couldn't find my fashion styles anywhere in the market. I didn't do it for pleasing people, but I guess it becomes part and parcel of it when you think about presenting yourself right. With time, I developed a strong relationship with one nearby tailor.

Her name was Sarah, and she was a woman with a long neck and thin shoulders who was the most receptive to my tailoring requests. She always knew what to do whenever I took my clothes there. I had only to speak, and she would begin nodding her head profusely as if the revelation came from up above. She had memorized my body size and her work always made me return gratified. I sometimes told her that if I become rich, I will make her my personal stylist.

My tailoring and fashion didn't amuse everyone always. One naysayer was my mother. She was always mad at me for buying something decent and taking it to tailors to alter it. I would return from Sarah, and she'd roll her eyes or frown. But for the most part, she decided to let me be. She complied with it more and more until she eventually got into the groove of my taste.

Eventually, my whole family started admiring my fashion sense. My mom had now begun appointing me to buy pretty clothes for my sister and brothers as well. She gave me my due, agreeing that I wear the nicest, simplest outfits. Everybody in the neighborhood knew that about me, but it was pleasant to listen to my mom say it. One thing my mom didn't seem to appreciate was that I liked mini dresses and miniskirts.

At that time, wearing mini dresses as a girl equated to only one thing. It meant that you were sexually active and that you were a slut. Whenever I passed by my neighbors, I would watch from the corner of my eye or hear them whispering from a distance, and I knew that they thought I was a slut. Again, it didn't bother me because deep down, I knew who I was. I was different, smart, respectful, very intelligent, and I liked what I liked. I knew that the impositions of society had brought many valuable selfhoods down and broken many people. I had to convince myself I was on the right track every day. It wasn't a picnic, though. It was challenging to raise a child like me in the environment we lived in, full of society's expectations and rules and norms and mores on how everyone should conduct themselves.

As for me, I lived by no one's rule but my own. I did whatever made sense to me. That was me, that was Josine. I had luckily discovered and explored who I was at a very young age, and so never let the outside world influence me. I never allowed society or anyone to set standards for me because I already had my own.

Soon, I gave my much-anticipated primary national exams. I already talked about the fact that the better your grades are, the higher your chances of admitting into a reputable high school. Now, those students who got with the least grades either joined the free public high schools or repeat the class. I wanted to join the best of the best Catholic high school for girls in the country. I really had much confidence that I will.

Every teacher visited our house the night before the national exams to wish me good luck. The amount of support and love that I received once again scared me all the more. I did not want to disappoint those who believed in me. However, the firmest believer in me was me myself.

On the day of the exam, my mom woke up very early in the morning and made me breakfast. It wasn't a breakfast meal. It was more like a morning lunch. She cooked such rich food that we usually ate for lunch. It did arouse my appetite, but after that, all I could think of was that the exam was going to determine my whole future. Everything hinged on it. It was the leap I was taking, and only after the jump was over that my fate was going to decide where I landed.

My future peaked at me from a corner. It was pushed to the corner out of my fear, but simultaneously in the center due to my confidence. I knew that if I failed, I was going to end up in primary public schools that can hardly get you a scholarship at the end of high school. Plus, I knew for a fact that my mom will not be able to pay for my college tuition. Imagine, a girl right after her elementary school worrying about her scholarship already. Not only worrying slightly but also striving for that.

It was a Monday evening when the national exam scores were announced. I had waited for that day with so much curiosity and so many palpitating heartbeats. I was so nervous that I sometimes got the words of my prayers wrong too. I couldn't eat. I was just hooked to the gate, impatiently waiting for my school teacher to bring our school results. And eventually, they did. They picked up their pace when they saw my worried face.

The envelope came crisp and white. It was supposed to hold the results of all the students in all the 100+ schools in our district. There was a good chance that I would have made somewhere in the upper percentile, but the fear that had gripped me then made me question if I would have passed even. It was a small voice, a small fear.

My mom held my hands as we slowly picked it out a very white list and checked for the national exam scores. I started from the middle and scoped my eyes like a sniper. My heart rose to my throat, and something burned in my legs. My name was at the top of the list... I was the top in my whole district, which had more than 100 schools. I leaped all two meters in the air, jumping and screaming with delight. It was unbelievable. I couldn't hold myself, as if bugs had crept into my blood. I burst into tears right away while I was laughing at the same time. It was for the first time I was feeling that proud of me. The entire memory reel of my journey passed by my eyes. I saw Congo, I saw the struggle, I saw suffering, I saw my dream and my dream breaking, I saw the hunger for education and striving for it. And there I was, top of the district.

Soon, hours later, the district leader called my family to tell them that they had rewards for me. This wasn't expected. I dressed in my usual fashionable clothes, and the happiness all came naturally to me. Ceremoniously, they awarded me a brand new smartphone, along with $30. Thirty dollars was a treasure for me back then. It was a lot of money. I only took $10 and gave the rest to my mom.

Being the top student in my district, and being a girl at that also qualified me for another award. The Rwandan First Lady presented it to me through the Imbuto Foundation Organization, which was a very high honor. They gave us more money and school materials too. These moments are one of the highlights of my life, among the proudest moments for my family and me.

And so started my high school journey after being allocated to one of the nearby priest boarding high school. It was an Art school called 'Ecole D' Art de Nyundo,' reputed to be among the best schools in my district. But it still was not what I had imagined. I was still not happy about it. I wanted to go to all women high school, the place where my best friend Rose was going. She was just as happy for my results when they arrived.

It was as if my happiness was her happiness. Her result was pretty impressive too, and thus she made it to a good high school. Rose's mom tried to talk to some of her connections for my sake because she also wanted us to go to the same boarding high school. Unfortunately, it didn't work out. I was upset at the time, but it's like they say, (wo)man plans and God laughs.

In my case, my high school was going to be where my beneficient blessings and successes lay hidden. I didn't know it at that time, but like they also say, *"everything happens for a reason."* This was a beautiful reason. Who knew what experiences awaited me had I gone to Rose's high school. One more interesting fact, 'Ecole D' Art de Nyundo' was happened to be the same high school that my dad went to also! When I learned about that from my mom, my eyes went wide. Such a coincidence! That made me feel better about where I was going. The best part about going to a boarding school, I discovered, was that your family would buy you a lot of stuff such as mattresses, toiletries, towels, bedsheets, a bucket, and other things that every school already had on their list. I mean, we had that at our own place too, but there was a greater delight, a more profound pleasure in owning all of those things as a young girl.

In preparation, my mom helped me pack my clothes and luggage. As I said goodbye to my brothers and neighbors, I realized I was about to spend three months in the boarding school away from them. I thought of my mother, too. It was a sudden realization that I figured three months was the longest I had ever spent away from home, away from those people. I secretly wiped my tears in my room and moved out.

My mom accompanied me to the new school. Unlike herself, she did not have an itinerary of instructions this time. She just gave me one piece of advice, *"Study hard,"* she said to me. She knew that was where my passion lay. She also knew, funnily enough, that no matter what she instructed me, I was going to do my own thing. I wish she knew that at that time, I would have given anything to listen to her set of instructions in that endearingly concerned manner she relays them. My mom's face was trembling as if she was making the greatest attempts to hide her emotions when we reached the gates of the school. I noticed the glimmer in her eyes, the shudder in her breath, and I looked away. Knew full well what would have happened if I didn't.

She didn't want to leave me but knew full well that she had to. In an instant, the warmth of her body was on mine. Tender and smelling intensely like her scent. She enveloped me very tightly, and I returned it with all my strength, nowhere able to match her strength. She whispered in my ears, *"May God be with you."* And then we both were shaking and wet with tears.

I could also see that she wanted to tell me that she loved me and that she was proud of me, but African parents rarely mention those statements. They will, on the other hand, show you how much they love you. They would show you all you wish to see in their love. But they will never tell you, that's just how it is. And I like it like that. Actions speak louder than words for me. Mother didn't have to mention her love because her words would've fallen short against what I saw in her eyes. It was one of the priceless moments of my life, the one I secretly photographed as a mental picture. Moving past the feels and tears now. So starting high school was a new thrill. I had new goals of studying harder than I ever did. Whatever came after the district level, I wanted that. I wished to maintain my grades to make my mom more proud and also to make myself proud.

My dad had made history at that same high school, and he was the brightest kid, as well. It only reaffirmed my faith in myself that I am indeed his daughter. It was unusually soon that everybody knew who I was. Perhaps not my style and my disposition, but they knew I was the brightest kid who was enrolled amongst them. Though I was an all-rounder, I was known for only one thing: academic excellence.

I wanted to prove to them that it's true. I wanted to maintain my reputation. I desired my performance to exclaim that 'I am who you think I am, so brace yourselves.' As you would have been able to tell from the attention I've given them in this book, I was never interested in boys. Whether it be boys who tried to talk to me or boys who admired from a distance. I only wanted to do well in school, and that was all. It may come as a surprise to you, but I wasn't the typical 'nerd' who dreams of mathematical equations and spends every waking hour studying. Apart from studying, I also enjoyed high school parties too. With mild training in dancing, I had found it to be a pleasurable activity. I loved to dance so much that I would occasionally dance like there was no tomorrow.

That's how the first semester went by, boys trying their luck on me, studying extensively, and enjoying high school parties. It went by so quickly, and yet again, I became the top student in my class. I worked for it and had earned it; it wasn't just genetics, in case you're wondering about that. And so I was starting to get comfortable with success in life.

During the holidays, I learned that there was a new international high school in Rwanda. I don't know if it was a friend who told me that or I read a flyer, but it captivated my attention. It was an American single high school named Gashora Girls Academy High School, and the staff members were all white people. Soon, everyone in my school was talking about that school. The downside was, we could only talk about it, for the school was too expensive and only for rich kids. And so everybody's, including mine, eyes were on scholarships. We learned that Gashora High School offers scholarships to only thirty students in the whole country. That means one student in every district. The good news was that the same American high school had offered a scholarship to one girl at my high school. She performed well in the entire district. I wasn't jealous, for she was two years ahead of me. The chances were still open for me.

I immediately started dreaming and praying about the admission in this premium high school. The only requirement they had was doing excellently in the O' level's (first three years of high school) national exam. This meant that I had to beat every girl in my district once again, which seemed so impossible. At the elementary level, it was more doable, I told myself. But the stakes and standards were higher here and now.

I would study nights and days now. Like a nerd, you can say that now. I so badly wanted to be admitted into that high school. I prayed like never before; I studied like never previously. None of my friends knew about my goal. They only found me absent from all the fun and games and parties. They did know that I must have been studying to get the highest grades in my class again. But I was no longer studying to be the topper in my class. My friends would sometimes jokingly say that I over study as if I'm being paid for it. It was in good humor, and so it never affected me. I had a goal to reach, regardless of being a girl of age 13. Time traveled like time again, quickly. Soon, I found myself taking my second national exam for which I had dedicated so many hours and sacrificed so much, for this was the moment of truth.

The review was going to determine if I make it into the new international high school or not. Despite my hard work, I was uncertain if I could get the admission. The competition was, after all, a little too much now. Gashora Girls Academy was the best high school in Rwanda. All the wealthy families were trying to get their kids in at any cost. All the successful students were studying hard to qualify for the scholarship. And there I was, falling amongst the latter.

I made the best of my efforts with studies. I went prepared, had the blessings of my mother on my head, and all the faith in my heart. I truly believed that God would do the rest after the efforts I make. To my astonishment, I was again the top student in my district. It was as if one by one, all my academic dreams were made to come true inevitably.

Or perhaps the universe was making up for the longest-term dream of how I had envisioned my home. I don't know. But either way, if I was jumping with glee back after the first time, I was flying after topping in my district the second time. They were selecting one student from every district, and I was the best in mine. I was awarded the scholarship. My family couldn't grow any more proud of me. My mother had grown so delirious for me that congratulating me felt beyond her. But her prayers had contributed direly.

This was not only a scholarship to me, but it was the resource I was to cash on for the longtime goal of going to college abroad. It was still a secret to me that I was weaving this new dream, though everyone used to tell me that I deserved it. My uncles and aunties would refer to me as 'American' because of my character and how different I was.

They just couldn't find how or what to classify me as, other than referring to me as an American. My aunties will also say to me that I should marry a white man because no African man is going to stand a woman like me. I did not have the passivity and submissiveness that an average man desires. They genuinely thought that I was a feminist. Feminism was quite uncommon in my society. Hereon, I was also mentally prepared for a different life. It was one I knew for sure that Rwanda was not going to offer to me. It wasn't the home I dreamed of, not the place I fit in. Being myself was a struggle among my own people. And so then I internalized my role. I was ready to face the disapprovals and disturbances with eloquence and wit.

Sometimes I responded to boys at my high school who was trying to get my attention that I'm marrying a French man for them to back off. I would keep a dead-serious face because I never felt like I belonged there anywhere. So they may judge me all they want. Come to think of it; I didn't know if I would have belonged in French society either. I wanted to believe that I might.

My teachers taught us France is an open-minded country that has a more flexible culture. Yet I doubted. I was, however, willing to explore other cultures on a journey to find myself on a deeper-rooted level. I loved the idea of passing by places, even if I wasn't settling there. In the end, I would have reached where I actually fit. So France was one of the places. I wanted to move to France for my college education. My exposure to Rose and her family heightened my interest in that. It sounded classy to me, fancy and romantic too. I dreamt about meeting a tall, blonde, French guy and getting married to him. I couldn't bring myself to imagine marrying a Rwandan boy. The impression ingrained in my mind was that they would want me to be a housewife. I did not for the life of me saw that happening. I wasn't what people typically called a 'wife material.' I was never one of them.

They described a wife material lady, like a woman who could cook, please her husband, keep the house clean, and produce children. To me, cleaning and cooking needn't any gender-oriented classification. Those are basics skills that each man and each woman should be able to do without holding a preference or pressure upon one side. I wanted someone who will see me more than just a woman who can cook, clean, and bare kids. I was ambitious, I had goals to achieve, and I had a fire in me and my individuality. Like a precious gem, I too yearned to be discovered.

My Journey at Gashora Girls Academy

The news spreads fast like wildfire. Everyone in the district has heard it. Josine Mutuyimana is going to the most expensive high school in the country. A celebrity status finds me, but I don't care about that too much. My mom was now the proudest in the village, and that was what mattered to me the most. As if the honors weren't enough, the school staff topped it all off by arriving at my door to pick me directly from home. Seeing white people with the shiny, pristine cars coming to pick me from home was like a scene from a movie.

A crowd had gathered, their mouths floating open. It seemed like everyone in the village was staring at us, murmuring, wondering what was going on in my family. The staff members from Gashora Girls Academy interviewed me on the spot. By that, I don't mean a fleeting interview. I mean with a camera and a microphone with a white woman on my face.

There were cameras set all over my place at home, and I felt like a superstar. I was stuffed with anxious confidence, overpowered by the pride I was feeling. It was amazing to be the center of attention, but also very uncomfortable. I couldn't speak English at all, but I was accommodated for that. I had a translator during my interview, again from the school's side. I had a whisper of a thought, where I wondered if I got into school or got selected for a role in a movie. They did the interview, wrapped it up, and sat me in the car. I still had not recovered from it all, yet off we flew. Before leaving, I hugged my siblings and my mother very tightly for the longest time. Rose was there too, along with her mom. I said goodbye to all of them, and they had nothing for me but good hopes and *"best of lucks"* and prayers for my success.

My life was about to change forever, I thought, as the scenes of the country passed by my car window. I also acknowledged that compared to all the previous times, the struggle ahead of me would be double the intensity. I knew that the school I was joining was only for the top students in the country.

There were other toppers of their districts, so this time, the competition was going to be more real than ever. We drove for six hours before we arrived at the school in the Kigali suburb. With all the buzz and excitement, being before cameras, bidding farewell to the village and my family, and all the thoughts during my travel, I grew tired. I cannot explain how curious I had been about the school. I would dream of how the building looked like; the classrooms, the gymnasium, and the staircases, everything. I was wondering about the appearance of the students and the quality of food too. A rumor went that the food over there was like hotel meals. The thought alone made my mouth water. I came to believe that the cafeteria and the washrooms would all be like hotel service pristine. And I wasn't disappointed.

I was greeted by jolly faces of senior girls helping the fresh-women check-in. At first glance, I could tell they were from elegant families and conditioned to be very prim and disciplined. They looked very beautiful, were soft-spoken, and almost all of them had long, well-taken-care-of hair. Those with short hair covered it up with their extra enchanting smiles.

The building was deluxe, built according to international standards. The angled or triangle roofs were corrugated, the color of pink sandstone. Beneath it stood the generous beige buildings of the campus. Everything looked new, recently constructed, and so premium that I had a nervousness growing inside of me. Despite that, I managed to stay calm and remained observant. Looking at other students pouring in, their parents dropping them, kissing their foreheads, snapping pictures with them, I realized how peasant, ugly and poor I might have looked. Everyone was talking to each other in fluent English. Bulleting words and lightning-quick responses. And then there was me, trying to figure out how I was going to survive with my arid English vocabulary. The first impression of the place was at once emphatic and dreadful. I spent the first whole night wondering which strategies I needed to use to get the most out of this school.

I was too scared to speak anything, for I would have embarrassed myself. It appeared as if I was the only minority and poor kid around. Something that had never happened was emerging to happen. I was growing too scared of the competition around the place. I had always been a topper, after all. I have never faced the threat of being overtaken.

Here, since I was witnessing how every student at the school was carefully selected, as if the best hand-picked peaches on a farm, and that they lived up to their potential, it was going to be the hardest battle I had to fight. In spite of these worries, the place exceeded my expectations, and I comforted myself with that. The school was beautiful with greenery all around. The uniforms, too, were very fancy. They cost $60, compared to the uniform at my former school that cost about $5. Everything about the school was overwhelming. I had never seen women as gorgeous as Gashora girls with their smooth, perfect, even skin. They all looked luxurious and classy. The food was the most fantastic thing about the academy. They had professional chefs who made the best and most fancy meals I have ever tasted. From Brochettes to pilau rice with salad on the side, Fried sweet potatoes to Pizza, we had it all.

I enjoyed it to the fill of my delight. Yet, needless to say, everything made me look very poor and helpless. I couldn't believe that even the school maids spoke better English than me. Who was I to be there? Struggling to belong, in a world of my own, I would keep asking myself the same question. The second morning at school, we had classes.

The classrooms were huge and neat, hinting a modern air about it. It was not the kind I had been used to in my previous schools. I didn't say a single word in any of my classes throughout the day. I did not even ask questions. I was too intimidated by my classmates' English proficiency and feared getting laughed at upon my clumsy and limited English words. I was starting to get convinced that I was in the wrong place. A huge internal battle was burgeoning in me. On the other hand, my family thought that I was so lucky to be admitted to the best high school in Rwanda. Knowing that made me more scared to disappoint them or even misuse the opportunity that I had. I was told during the orientation that if I don't perform well, my scholarship will be taken away. The fear set its roots so deep in me that I cried almost every day in my first week at school. I had no friends, no one in the whole world to express my catharsis.

I was not able to ask questions in class. It made me feel invisible. Add to that, I was among the few students from low-income families at school, probably the poorest among all. Whenever I would look at my face in the mirror, I saw a girl whose eyes were crying for help. There was no one to help me. I had been in the wild and more at peace than I was among the most civilized and all the wonderful privileges.

All these thoughts stormed in my head, and eventually, I got depressed. I buried myself in my own feelings and thoughts; went around like a zombie. I felt so lonely, for the most part. I sometimes couldn't even find myself to be there for me. Yet, I had to strengthen myself up. I have learned to see obstacles as opportunities in my life. And so, sitting at my own tiny bed one day, I wiped my tears furiously and said to myself, *"Enough is enough."* I reminded myself how far I have come, how hard I have worked to reach where I am today. I replayed the battles I fought and picked on newfound courage that was brewing. In that instant, I made a decision that I was going to be myself regardless. I realized that I had been bothered by the fact that I didn't fit in my new community.

Then I thought, have I ever anywhere? I questioned myself if I really had to. I made up my mind that I'm never going to fit in, but I'm going to survive because this is precisely the school I prayed and worked so hard for. If God brought me here, there was a purpose to it. I wasn't going to squander it. I reminded myself that I was different and that I should embrace my differences instead of trying to fit in.

"I was raised differently, and that's just who I am," I would whisper to myself. I also decided to at least learn three English words per day and to ask questions in class regardless of my broken English. If someone was to laugh, they may. I wished to use humiliation as my motivation and strength. I was there to win, after all. Not to lose. Winning is never easy. It takes getting out of your comfort zone and going the extra mile.

With the new courage, I started reading books and asking as many questions as I could. It turned out that everyone had something to say about my accent and how I pronounce R as L, but I refused to care. It was like I was back at mom's hometown again. Some of my teachers could easily spot the differences between my classmates and me. It was right there in their eyes, that pity they would feel for me, which also drove them to help me even more.

I needed the help, so I didn't mind. Especially since they were compassionate, I made the most of it. The school had different clubs, and students were hungry to become club leaders. It was a huge race, a fight. Everybody wanted a leadership position at school, and at first, I didn't understand why. I later realized that they were trying to build their resumes because they were planning to apply to American universities.

I was a passive girl in the eye of the tornado with a circling rat race around me. I didn't know what a resume was at that time, silly as that may sound; thus, I didn't know what the competition was all about. Plus, I was not going to compete anyway. My job was to study and excel academically. That was a difficult enough task, for the

Gashora girls were very competitive in everything they did. Something I had never seen elsewhere. The girls knew what they wanted, and they would do anything to get it. Some would try to be friends with school staff, visiting their offices more often just to put their names out there. Others were invested in SAT preps. Another trope was fighting for leadership positions. Some of them had parents who made sure that the school principal knows their kids.

Then there were several just like me, trying to survive, one foot in front of the other. The rest were all about their interests and goals. The environment was that of a pressure cooker, hotter than a regular school. As for me, I was low-key trying to keep my scholarship at that point in time. I dropped the idea of going to study abroad by just looking at the competition, and how qualified those women were compare to me. There was no way I would make it, I thought.

When I resolved to remain myself, life at Gashora was starting to ease out. The creases of doubts, such as my identity and my origins, remained hidden. Nobody found out, nor was curious. It always meant lowered chances for embarrassing myself. Almost all of the other students had come from well-known families in the country. Among them, if I was a nobody, why not then act like it too? And so I did. I became a nobody no one bothered to want to know about. Yet, halfway through my first semester, I made a friend named Giella. With all my endeavors to be a nobody, how come I made a friend, you might be presuming? The answer lies in who Giella was.

She was one of the most devil-may-care girls in the entire school. So carefree, she was that she was mostly sleeping during class lectures. That's what she was known because of her sleeping in class. She loved to sleep so much, and she dodged morning preps and evening preps just to stay in bed. Needless to say, Giella was a dreamer. She lived in a world of her own making where her leisures were daydreaming, and her life was all about fantasy dreams.

You would always find her with a novel in her hands. This bibliophile would be sleeping, and even then, a novel would be in her hands. Nothing in the world bothered Giella. It was awe-striking to see that she was also one of the rich kids, but she never acted like one. Her skin smoothness and subtle etiquettes, like how primly she ate her food, couldn't hide where she was from, but that didn't matter when it came to her temperament.

I, who had been preparing for a friendless high school journey, didn't imagine that I would come to have a lifelong best friend such as Giella. I connected with her. Despite our family income differences, we had a lot in common. We both lived in our fantasy world, kept to ourselves minding our businesses, and both lived like no one was watching. We had our goals with which we refreshed our souls daily, keeping them close to our hearts.

Even if we did not look like girls who had dreams – in Giella's case, the sleeping ones do not count – but we not only had them but were chasing them in our own ways too. We would laugh about the competition between Gashora girls and how some girls try way too hard to be relevant. I hadn't forgotten my madness for competition myself, but for me, it was more about my personal achievement, reflecting my potentials rather than being keen on stepping over another person. Some of the girls fell among the latter.

That did not mean that Giella and I weren't studying hard. I would make notes in class and my free time. One night before the exam, I would lend Giella my notes, and that would be the only time she would stay up for evening preps. And like that, we became closer and closer every day. Time went by quickly. Class after class, week after week, exam after exam. Somewhere between these transitions, the tightening of my muscles released. Against the odds, I was starting to get used to the school and school life. We had one day allocated for relatives and family members visiting us. My sister came to visit me for the first visiting day. I anticipated her with yearning because there was so much that I wanted to share with her.

I couldn't wait to tell her about the troubles, befriending Giella, the mad stupid competition. She couldn't wait to hear about it either. And so when we met, we were like two giggling schoolgirls brimming with glee and gossip. I took her around the school, too, giving her an elaborate tour. For me, her coming was more than a visit. There was a sense of ownership I had started feeling towards the school, so I showed her around as if I was the president.

On top of that, as I have mentioned, I so very badly needed to meet and talk to somebody about my school struggles and life at Gashora Girls academy. Someone who understood me, who would not judge me. My sister was that ideal person. She was at the same frequency as me. She listened to me patiently and knew just what I needed to hear.

Imagine a sandbag, or an anchor, finally released from a balloon or a ship. That was how I felt after that meeting with my sister. Our school offered lunch for visitors. That day, our lunch was bread with peanut butter, some cold beverages, and beef sandwiches. I loved bread so much, especially at school. There was magic in our bakers' hands, as they made the most delicious bread in all of Rwanda. My sister and I took every bite of it for the precious entity it was.

The visiting day also functioned as a day to show off for most affluent families at the academy. Gashora boasted not one of, but *the* richest kids in the country. They belonged to the most elite families of very influential persons you would see on the TV. They seemed to know each other, and that was why the show-off competition was more than fiery.

It was also treated as a networking event whereby rich people who did not know each other met one another and became friends through their kids. And then the usual boasting followed; my kid this, her achievements that, the medals, the trophies, the certificates, and yadda-yadda. Rich people brag about their kids like their life depends on it. What was excruciating was that it would be subtle, yet each would know just what they are doing – one-upping the other.

Respective daughters represented every family, and they all wanted to win. It was funny. They competed to talk to the school principal, or the university counselor, coaxing their way around to win scholarships or more scholarships. And then there was me, on the other hand, sitting on the tiny bed for hours with the blissful sight of my sister before me, talking for hours. Believe it or not, that was everything to me. That simplicity made it an even more memorable day for me.

In the middle of the first semester, we used to have a weekly assembly where the student journalists presented trending news at school. At its end, the school principal would also give out official announcements. Most of the time, the school invited guest speakers. They would be the ribbon-cutters, the introductory speech-givers of the during the school assembly.

The first time, we had the founder of the school as the special visiting guest, and it was indeed a special assembly, which also turned out to be the worst day of my life at Gashora Girls Academy. All was going smoothly, the founder spoke, the journalists came, and the principal spoke, and then strangely, the founder's turn came again at the end.

He had a speech to make about how the school was founded. The school staff had put together videos that showed the journey the school went through to reach the point where it was at. You might be thinking about what could possibly follow that made it be my worst day at school, right? Well, as it so happened, one of the videos happened to be my video. And which video was it? It was the video that was taken when they came to pick me up from home.

I had not known their intentions when they offered me a ride to school on my first day. One thing I did not mention earlier was that when they had gotten inside the house, along with the interview, they had also asked me something else. They wanted to make a little video scene where I would be with my mom doing the house chores and acting like myself at home. I had to specifically wear dirty clothes that I used to wear while doing the house chores.

The same went for my mom. It was part of the directions of the video. And so, we pretended to act like we were cooking by peeling potatoes and by having the conversations that they instructed us to have. This angle and that, they surrounded us. They wanted me and my mom to talk about the new opportunity that I had just gotten and what it meant for us. Particularly, my mom had to remind me that I was an orphan. Yes, you heard that right. I had to use that shortcoming as a chance to change my family's life. I never liked to talk about my past outside my family. I did not like sharing about my passed-away dad. Not to Rose, not to Giella. I had not talked about it to anyone, but there I was on the screen, talking about just those things; I had to follow the script.

It was one of the hardest interviews I had given to date. It felt awkward and harassing, but I did not give it much thought once it was over. I should have sensed the disturbance in my intuition right away, but oh well. At least it was behind me, I thought. Yes, I never thought I would come across the interview again in my life. I was very grateful for the scholarship they gave me, and so while giving it and following the script, I had thought it was fair to let them film my poor family.

The intention was to use it for fundraising in the USA, they told us. I never knew they would show it in the assembly like that. It was unethical and immoral on so many levels because I was not informed about it either. They had filmed my whole house, my bed, my neighborhood, and all of that was displayed on the screen. Everything showed nothing but poverty. We were poor, yes, but I was not ready to expose my life to the world, especially not to Gashora girls. They would never understand the maturity and the lessons being poor, living in the wild, migrating the way I did result in. But there it all was, on the screen. I never felt betrayed in my life as I felt during the assembly. They should have consulted me before exposing my life, to which I would have never permitted, and then that little movie would have gone into oblivion for me.

The transition between the lavish scenes that preceded until my movie was jarring. I was pleased and unsuspectingly watched the Gashora academy journey until I saw my name and my face. Such horror filled me. It was as if my heart was stung, my lungs punctured. When I saw the movie introduction that announced my name out, I felt stabbed and turned my head down with my eyes closed, hoping that when I open my eyes, it would all just be a dream. Except that it wasn't. We all have been through moments like that, haven't we? Life hands us all our proportions of lemons, doesn't it? This was my moment.

I couldn't bear to watch myself and my life in front of everyone. I kept my eyes closed the entire time. Even then I couldn't escape the sounds and the automatic visuals my mind was forging. I was simply not ready for any of it. I had been struggling with trying to navigate my life at Gashora, trying to stay invisible with my poor English. Before that video started playing, I was an unknown, mysterious child, but at least no one knew where I was from or how poor I was.

I kept the guard up so well that not even Giella knew about it. I never talked about my family or my hometown or my history. I wanted to be invisible, seek education and graduate from that place. That was all. But there I was, exposing it all. Wrongfully, I hated myself at that moment too.

Everyone in the room had seemed to grow very quiet while watching my poor life. The girls that stood to my sides, I could feel them looking at me from the corner of their eyes. They were all so amazed by how poor my family is and the conditions that I lived in. It made them watch it all with even more attention and intently. That just made it worse. I honestly never felt humiliated as I had felt at that moment.

My heart and I were just waiting for it to be over, so we run into my room and cry. At the end of the assembly, that's what I did. I went straight to bed and wished to disappear more than ever, only to wake up when everybody had forgotten all about me. I cried, more like burst with every sob, wishing the earth would draw open and swallow me. At the same time, I was dazed. I couldn't believe what had just happened to me. Believe me or not, I felt naked.

I had never wished to die as I did at that moment. It doesn't entirely make sense why I felt that poignantly in that way over just a movie, right? It may have been just a movie to everybody else, but it was public molestation to me. It was rubbing salt in my wounds. It was a reminder that I don't belong or fit in the community I had earned to be in. It was also a reminder of my past that I never felt comfortable sharing with anyone. It was NOT just a movie.

I cried hysterically until I finally fell asleep. When I woke up, I couldn't eat for the rest of the day. I couldn't join others for the evening prep. I was so ashamed to face my classmates and everybody else at school that I entertained skipping all my classes and staying right there in my room. I would have taken notes for Giella, which was fine. Giella came to check up on me that night, but I pretended to be asleep because I didn't know what to say to her. For some reason, I also did not want to hear what she may have to say. Somehow, I felt like I owed everyone an explanation as to why I was very poor. I spent my night thinking about how I was ever going to get over this and what everybody else would be saying about me. But guess what the truth was? No one was talking about me. That was still fine. No one was making fun of me, but they all felt sorry and pity for me. Now that was still bad.

I had lived like I didn't have a past, and pity was not something I had required even if I had gotten to open that Pandora's Box. I was determined to leave everything behind the moment we came back to Rwanda from the Democratic Republic of Congo. Start fresh, start anew. But then again, until you accept that you have had a difficult past and get to the point where you can boldly talk about it, you will never be able to move on. It will continue to hold you back.

I soon somehow felt relieved that everyone knew who I was despite the pity. I found some kindness in the eyes of the richer girls too. They stopped judging me for my poor English. My professor showed much more empathy towards me and extended tolerance during my classes. Some of them reached out and told me to feel free to ask them for help regarding anything. One of them, my chemistry professor, who also happened to be my advisor, wrote me a note telling me how brave and strong I was for bearing and fighting through all that I did. He assured me that the future is definitely going to be bright. That upward social mobility awaited me. He ended with a motivating quote that brought my spirits up. If you find yourself saying, *"But I can't speak English,"* *try adding the word, "...Yet".*

That just was everything I needed to hear at that moment. My professor, to this day, may not have had any idea how wonderfully he helped me, but he truly did. I felt stronger than before. Remembering my old habits, I immediately started writing my new goals and how I was going to put the movie far behind me. I was going to strive to achieve everything that I wanted to get out of Gashora Girls Academy. I wrote, and I wrote and I until I concluded that the movie doesn't define me, and I was never defined by my past, which did, however, molded me. And this was only the next day of the assembly. Due to my will and my professor's uplifting words, what should have been the most humiliating afternoon turned out to be a new beginning for me, my new motivation. I decided to own my past and use it as my fuel to soar higher. I looked back only to realize how unique my journey had been to others. They were spoon-fed luxuries. I had to go to extra lengths to earn basic necessities. I had fought to be where I was at that moment. And there I was, smiling down at the notepad I had filled. There I was, picking myself up again.

Thus, like all things, all was well that ended well.

The first semester went by so fast, and luckily enough, I did academically well. I was able to maintain my scholarship for the next semester, which was all that I had worked for. Surviving the first semester also meant that I would survive the next one. The end of the semester asserted there was hope for me. Another lucky fact is that at that point, my family was no longer pressuring me about my grade. They didn't even ask for it. They knew I did well and must have done what I could in an environment such as that. Yet, I somehow felt the need to remind them to ask me about my transcripts.

When I returned home, my mom was elated to see me after my first semester from American high school.

During my third semester, a scholarship opportunity came by, and I was one of the candidates who were encouraged to apply. The selected candidates would go to a South African International High School called African leadership Academy, said to be one of the greatest high schools for intelligent and hardworking students. Unlike previous times, it brought out not the best students from a district of the country. Rather, it brought the best high school students from all over Africa.

The scholarship had some conditions, of course. In order to be eligible, you had to be coming from a low-income family and have remarkable grades, undoubtedly so. Learning about it excited me. I thought that it was a wonderful opportunity for me, and I had hopes that I might get in.

In preparation, I started reading English books to improve my speaking skills and grammar. Assured of my passion, the school principal had agreed to edit my essays. He knew me as the girl from the school movie. I started the application process, and I passed the first round, which they called the screening process. Myself and five other students were invited for an interview, out of which only three students were going to be shortlisted. I prayed so hard for my acceptance, and I truly believed that I had a chance to get in. I knew that also meant I would have more competition than ever since my school had the brightest students from all over Africa. It was going to be a strict and the most nail-biting challenge for me. The stakes were higher, too, for it was part of the question of my journey ahead.

The interview lasted for three hours and was divided into three sessions. I did my best, but I realized that I had not done well enough. It was my first time experiencing a college-level application, and I was at least grateful for that as it opened my mind to it. At the end of the day, I didn't get admission. Yes, I was crestfallen, since I had put a lot of effort into it. I didn't let the emotions overtake me. I didn't wallow in it. It was one of those rare moments of my failure, but I knew I had to experience it.

I was glad about the experience, for it inspired me to start thinking about applying for college abroad. I had gained so much confidence from the process. I learned about my mistakes and from them, which I was keen to amend for the next time, and I learned about my plus points too. The school had shortlisted me as one of the finalists from among a beautiful lot. And so I was optimistic. Little by little, people started getting to know me, and not only because I was from a low-income family. At the end of every academic year, my school held a public speaking competition. Giella and I would brag about going to join one. It was more like a joke, but as we walked by the registration office, we decided what could be the loss in it? And like that, we signed up for the public speaking competition in jest.

We always wanted to do things out of curiosity and impulse, so that was one experience ticked off. I had no intention to compete, especially not with the very articulate Gashora girls with their American accent. I just wanted experience. The public speaking competition was divided into three sessions. In the first session, you had to present a speech that was three minutes long in front of four judges.

In the second session, you had to present a four-minute speech in front of ten judges. The last session required you to present a five-minute speech in front of the whole school, including the honorary guests. Still out of curiosity and as entertainment, Giella and I practiced together multiple times before the first round. We would pose and laugh about it because we had never planned the whole thing in the first place. We could have easily backed out just before it happened even, so it was no big deal. Yet, it was really tempting an opportunity for me to practice my English. Believe it or not, we went through and eventually passed the first round. They invited us for the second round, and we were nearly laughing. It was still a joke for us. Lesser than before, but a joke nonetheless. We again practiced extensively for the second round. This was where it suddenly stopped becoming a joke.

We had surprisingly won again. They announced our names and handed us a ticket to the final round. There we were, dazed and looking at each other. It was no longer a joke. It was real. We now had to prepare for and present a speech that was going to be five minutes long. We would be standing not in front of five or ten people, but the entire school's eyes will be on us, along with the guests.

The public speaking competition had started with thirty competitors, and only five of them made it to the final round. My best friend and I were one of the five, the five of the best in the school. This time, I wanted to win. Out of those five, I wanted to be the number one this time. It had been a joke before, but now I was going to treat it as a competition, presenting before almost five hundred people. First of all, true, it was an achievement to be among the finalists. I had to stop and congratulate myself, as well as my friend, first before gulping all that pressure again. I was now going to compete against my best friend rather than alongside her. I may have been competing against the other debaters, but for the final round, I was rooting for Giella who, in turn, was rooting for me.

Nobody would ever believe that I would make it to the final round. Of course, even I wasn't. People expected less from me, and you can say that I expected lesser from me. I was that flimsy English speaking girl who used to pause a lot. To conceive then that I would be debating, it was insane. Not just that, that I would be thriving in it? It was flabbergasting.

I practiced again with Giella, from speeches to choosing the outfit for that special event, all. I was always intimidated by my fellow girls' English proficiency, and I had practiced for my own too. Everyone at school admired students who spoke English very well, especially with an American accent. I, of course, did not have that but didn't make any efforts to gain it either.

As the day of the competition approached, I was ready, and I had practiced multiple times. I hugged my best friend, both dressed in our best, and we wished each other good luck. I wanted her to win because even here, I wasn't entirely expecting to win. They normally say that practice makes perfect. I had practiced repeatedly, too hard, perhaps, sometimes sacrificing my food and sleep over it. But was it going to be enough? Only those five minutes in front of more than five hundred people could tell.

Practice makes perfect seemed to have worked just fine for me. My speech had gotten everybody quiet and amused. A sheer silence fell upon the hall for the first few seconds. I know I was the girl from the video before them. They had expected lesser from me. By then, there must have passed just nine months at the school, imagine, nine months learning English, nine months at Gashora Girls Academy.

Yet, I did not doubt that my speech, in writing, was one of the best speeches. I just had to make the delivery right when I presented it. I was full of confidence when I went there and spoke. I couldn't recognize that it was me. After that brief instant of silence after the end of my speech, everybody stood up and gave me a round of applause that reverberated in my heart. It was obvious that I won from that act alone. And I had indeed won. I had won the Public Speaking competition at Gashora Girls Academy, and it was so prideful an achievement that I celebrated the whole night. My name was now becoming known for graceful things, first, the scholarship finalizer and then the winner of this competition. Everybody respected my hustle. Students who never spoke to me approached me to congratulated me. For the first time in my life, perhaps, I was starting to feel a little sense of belonging.

In that very semester, fuelled by my encouragement for applications, I applied for the American Peace Corps over the school break. I wanted to use every opportunity to learn English by spending time with English speakers, but I also wanted to volunteer. I spent my Christmas break working with the American Peace Corps in one of the villages.

There I educated young women about HIV AIDS and contraceptive methods. Everything that I was doing, as it would later turn out, was building up my resume as a high school student. I didn't even know about it at the time, but it would help work things out for me in the future. I had never thought about the resume thing. What would I think about?

I knew that it was for people applying for jobs, and that meant university graduates in my country. That life was still far from me. I would have seen it when the time would come for it. As my academic life was flourishing, so did my social life, eventually. I was now talking to some boys outside the school and was even considering getting a boyfriend. It felt like a good distraction for me, for I had grown accustomed to spending too much time studying. I had grown to like boys by then, but I was too scared... to get pregnant by them. Although I knew that I was never going to have sex with anyone any time before I finish university, I was still scared for some reason.

Perhaps it was because anything that seemed like it could become a potential distraction for my future. It scared me to death. I had this deep-seated worry that anything can prevent me from achieving everything I promised myself to accomplish if I let that thing take over me. I wasn't going to let my dreams squander like that. I had dreams, among which buying my family a house was at the top. The second was making my mom proud along every part of my journey. As much as I wanted a boyfriend, I had to reconsider it. So then I came up with a fair middle way.

I laid down some rules or conditions in my head. There would never be any physical contact. I literally thought that I might get pregnant just by kissing a boy. I had once asked my mother what she thought about young women who accidentally get pregnant, just out of sheer curiosity. My mom replied by telling me if any of her daughters got pregnant like that, they should find another mother in place of her. I remembered that statement at Gashora, and it would make me think twice about opposite-sex relationships. However, I also wanted to prove to myself that I can get a boyfriend. It became like a dare to myself. I knew I was good enough, in both appearance and personality. But there was something that made me doubt.

Ever since I had turned twelve years old, I developed teenage cyclic acne that messed up my face and made me feel insecure about myself. I distinctly remember the time my classmates teased me when my face started breaking out for the first time. I had never wavered in my self-confidence about my looks. But that teasing bout made me feel less confident about myself to the extent where I started thinking that there is something wrong with my face.

My mom would bring me different lotions almost every month to help me with my skin, but the lotions made my situation worse. It would irritate or just make it uglier somehow. I wished somebody would have told me that cyclic acne was a normal part of growing up – because it didn't seem normal to me. What made my situation even worse was when people in the village started telling me that my face had been poisoned. I needed to seek medication from traditional doctors; they would tell me. And poor me, I would stress out about it.

After nearly the first two years of my acne face experience, I started growing in the hope that there will not be acne on my face anymore soon. I felt like it was going to disappear, and I had given up the thought that it was poison. But my mom… she had started buying the idea that my face had been poisoned. Our neighbors had told her that there are people who are jealous of her kids, especially the bright kid that I was, and my mom had started thinking that they poisoned my face because of being jealous of my success. This belief in the superstitious was commonplace in the village. Whenever somebody would fall sick, the first place where everyone's mind would fly off to shall be towards poison or witchcraft. They would immediately and reflexively rush over to seek medication from traditional healers and church pastors, who were considered to be as the doctors from God. This was the case among educated and uneducated alike. So, my mom started talking to me about going to church and having a pastor pray for my face. She later on invited two women who were 'prophets.' Women such as these would tell you everything to lead a certain event or thing up to its present point and what is going to happen. They are like time-seers or –profilers.

And so they came up to me, studied me with their wide eyes. The women started telling all of us to confess our sins. They then read the bible for us and prayed for us. In the middle of the prayer, one of them touched my face and said that I would receive healing in the name of Jesus. She asked my mom to bring a bottle of water so that she can bless it, and I was supposed to wash my face with that blessed water.

You must be wondering about my thoughts regarding all of these scenarios. Given that I was studying at a reputable school and was getting a world-class education, my mind wasn't completely and concretely set on any one thing. One part of me believed that this was going to work magic. Yes, a part of me thought that I was going to have a baby skin immediately after washing my face with that 'holy water.' Desperate times call for desperate measures, and I had both of them. I wanted my face clear now. I had grown extremely tired of everyone having something to say about my face and wasn't going to have any of it. As the women left our home, I couldn't wait to wash my face with the blessed water. There was an equal proportion of excitement and anxiety in me.

I dashed into the bathroom and washed my face elaborately. I then covered my face with a towel, wiped it very slowly and carefully, and did not remove the towel. After that, I inched my face closer to the mirror. I realized that my doubts had gone, and no, not on the intellectual axis, but I was expecting healing through and through. I was waiting for the big moment of looking myself in the mirror and seeing a clear baby skin with zero pimples.

That nervous excitement clung to me, and I said a short prayer before looking at myself in the mirror. How do I tell you, I really badly wanted that moment to be miraculous and prophetic and magical. I slowly removed the towel to see my face, and you may think I was watching my face as if after plastic surgery or something. I pulled my mirror right in front of my face… only to find out that my face was still the same. Nothing had changed, not one spot. I had my face memorized by then, and so could tell *nothing* had changed. I was sharply disappointed by what I by the results and discovered that there was no cure for my pimples. After that, I laughed at myself for even believing that simply normal water was going to do miracles to my face. Ridiculous.

Next, I tried to accept the fact that I have to live with my acne and that my face will be like that if not forever, then for a long, long time. But there was still one side of me that believed my face would be clear one day soon. Five years had passed, and my face was always the same. And so was my share of hope and despondency. But the latter was growing, of course.

My skin was breaking out every day, especially during my ovulation. People were commenting on it regularly. I was bothered by them, students who would always comment on my face by suggesting remedies and lotions and soaps that I should use to clear my skin as if I wouldn't have tried them myself. Everyone had something to say about my skin without me inviting them to. I know that they were trying to help and be polite, but it hurt me so much. It was something out of my control, something I couldn't escape. And to be reminded of it repeatedly, and to be the center of attention only because of my ugly skin. It was heinous. What could I do, I couldn't go around wearing a mask, could I? So I resorted to crying. I would cry at least twice a week because of my skin, and I actually believed that it was worse than it was. Like that video in the assembly, I guess.

I had tried almost everything everyone had recommended. Everything that I should have tried to clear my face, I had tried it all. Yet there were rare occasions when they would prescribe fresh remedies. Even though I acted like I didn't care whenever someone suggested some new cures, I would keep my pocket money and use it to buy expensive soaps and lotions, hoping that they would help me. But would they help? No sir. It was a blow after blow for me.

Things got worse when I turned 17. If I liked someone, especially some boy, I would refrain from looking at them directly in the face when I talked to them because I had this little voice inside me, always suggesting that they are staring at my acne and not my pretty smile or dimple. I tried to keep my eyes lowered in my interactions with the boys I was interested in. I tended to believed that I did not deserve someone to love me because of my skin. How ridiculous does that sound now? But that immaturity is a part of each of us when growing up. Similarly, I was in complete agreement that my face was ugly; therefore, I focused on improving other parts of my body. My waist, for example, was one, and I made sure that it was kept super slim. I started working out a lot to stay in shape since it was the only thing I thought will save me, the only thing under my control.

I started becoming conscious about what I ate and chose to eat healthy food only instead of junk or food full of carbs. I would wake up and do push-ups and ab exercises such as crunches before taking a shower. I made sure that my figure stayed on point, which it did. That raised my confidence, and so I resorted to controlling my self-confidence in myself like that.

That still did not mean I was going to stop thinking about my acne. It was still there, and still a grave cause of my worry. One day my biology teacher was teaching us about acids and bases. He mentioned that urine could balance the PH of the skin, and that makes it an excellent cure for acne. That electrified me. I picked on that, and believe it or not, started rubbing urine on my face before sleep. Don't ask me how or what of it. I just did it for two weeks, and nothing changed, so I stopped doing it. That was the end of it. I would always get annoyed whenever someone would suggest something that I should do to get a clear skin, which I would secretly consider and put that remedy to use but to no avail. In fact, I think I messed up my skin even more as a result.

Getting clear skin became almost impossible, and I eventually wanted to prove to myself that I am loved regardless. So we were back at that point of me wanting a boyfriend. The desire emerged from the drive to prove to myself that I can still get a man regardless of my skin condition.

One thing that did not change despite my skin condition was my high standards when it came to dating. I was still aware that I am an intelligent, goal-oriented woman who deserves nothing but the best. So, bad skin or not, I wanted a full-fledged, all-rounder handsome kind of a guy. I was aware I had an attractive body, a slim waist, and I knew I was fun, calm, and studious. My face was one exception, but so what. That didn't mean I was compromising on anything less.

And so time passed, and I got my first boyfriend when I turned 18. You already know there were no boys at Gashora, so we this guy and I met at one of my uncle's wedding. Since I also happened to be a good dancer, I had earned a reputation of being riveting. Everyone knew of me at the end of the wedding.

I spotted this man, another dancer, who was very flexible, had a distinct way of carrying himself, and seemed to have a fun personality with great dance moves. I had a thing for men who could dance since music was a big part of my life. Something about moving in harmony with the melody and beats instilled vigor in me. We got to talking at the wedding and then started dating a few months after.

As you should recall, I had certain ground rules pre-set in my mind when it came to dating and relationships. I made them evident to him, setting them forth, including the one that we can't kiss because I have a future waiting for me. I told him of my dreams that I had to follow and that I can't mess that up at any cost. Never for a boy. So, he would only kiss me on my forehead, and maybe a casual peck kiss here and there once in a while.

He was very respectful towards me and treated me like a valued possession, but I still had some insecurities on my part. Like especially when he tried to kiss my cheeks with acne on them or my forehead with acne, I would feel bad, and I would make him stop kissing me there like that. At first, it was reflexive. But then I would ask myself why he doesn't mind kissing my acne face. I figured perhaps the answer was because, in reality, my face was not as bad as I thought it was. I thought back to all those times when things weren't as bad as my mind had made them and figured this could be one of those.

My first boyfriend was really a validation for me to prove to myself that I can get any man I wanted regardless of my acne. I was successful, yes, but I didn't stop there. I had to prove it to myself again and again until I ended up realizing that acne has nothing to do with my love life.

Having to deal with acne skin, I went on a personal bout carrying out more detailed research on the surface so that I could understand better the underlying phenomena behind acne-ridden skin. Since all the medicine that others had prescribed failed me, I was going to find the root of it all myself. It became like a detective case for me, the skin became my crime scene, and the acne became my victim. After investigation, I learned so much about my skin. I came to understand what my skin type was and why I had breakouts. I slowly learned how to handle and manage my skin and mastered my seasonal breakout. I did it in the following manner. When I was getting my periods or ovulation breakout, a hormonal fiasco went underneath my skin. My acne was more like hormonal acne, which I couldn't fight easily. The only thing under my control was keeping my skin as clean as I could. That also included eating clean and working out. Part of the skincare regime also was accepted with peace the fact that some people just have sensitive skin.

I stumbled upon and learned about deep skin cleansing, such as using vitamin C containing skin cleansing solutions. It was more synthetic for my taste, so I resorted to going natural with everything. My vitamin C solution included using lemon water and Vaseline on my skin. That was the physical remedy. As for the psychological remedy, I changed my perception about my face, focusing on other great features, such as my smile.

During that period, I started falling in love with myself all over again after eight years of trying to fight acne with no success. I found it amusing and took it in good humor that I was unique in everything, including the fact that everyone in my family had the clearest skin I have ever seen except me. Among the many battles I fought, this one was going to be another, and I embraced it. It was comforting to think that unlike other members of my family, immediate and extended both, and I was blessed with premium quality education. In that light, the compensation I was paying through my skin was a fair enough deal.

With the last year of my high school in tow, our school-university advisor approached me and told me that I might be qualified to apply for some of the scholarships that help academically excellent students from low-income families. One of those scholarships was the MasterCard Foundation Scholarship that was at that time providing fully-funded scholarships to students from Sub-Saharan Africa. They were taking these students to American Universities. It captured my attention greatly. As always, the scholarship was very competitive, and they would only take like 15 students from all over Africa.

The university advisor recommended that I study for the SAT and TOEFL in order to apply. You can imagine that I didn't know what those exams were. My main focus at that time had been studying for the national exam Rwandan students had to take in order to be qualified for a Rwandan university scholarship. It was higher on the priority list. But I knew one thing was certain. My only way to go to college was going to come through getting a full scholarship, and I knew that I had it in me to do it.

Not residing in confusion, I took the more difficult approach. Four months before my high school graduation, I started giving my SAT and TOEFL preparation as well as simultaneously preparing for my national exam. Both of these were due in the same month as SAT and TOEFL. I was under pressure to do well in all three, especially since my school was paying for my SAT and TOEFL exams.

I did not want to disappoint them, but I also did not want to put all my concentration on those international exams and leave out the national one just in case I don't get in the university abroad. If not international, then I would still at least have my national scholarship to back me up. I have always been a woman with contingency plans, and that wasn't going to change this time around. If anything, it was going to intensify. When it came to planning for my college education, I had four plans. Plan A being applying for a MasterCard scholarship to go to US universities; plan B was applying for another full scholarship to study in South Africa; Plan C was applying for Kepler University that had a branch in Rwanda and was granting full scholarships to Rwandan students; lastly, plan D was to apply to Rwanda's national universities. I was going to put equal efforts in all of my plans since I was unsure which one of these would ultimately work.

As the SAT exam approached, I got a severe headache, which morphed and traveled down to become a stomachache. This stomachache was going to become a living hell in my life. I started to lose all my appetite and energy. I didn't know what I was suffering from. Things became very serious, and my stomach started to swell and grow large within a week. I decided to take a leave from school one day and went home to visit a doctor. I had agonizing pain in my stomach, in my back, and a head-squeezing headache that felt as if somebody was pressing it from the two sides using anvils. I had been forcing myself to study until I got to a point where I just couldn't anymore. The mysterious pain became extremely crippling. Add to that the fear of failure, which started running through my veins. In that headspace, in that phase, I couldn't think of any disease that caused an excruciating amount of pain as I was experiencing then.

I mean extreme pain is one thing, be it mysterious, but at such an inconvenient time? As if it hadn't been enough, the timing of my sickness started to make me sicker. I thought I had no more limit to take it anymore. Yet I had to push myself to do something. Surrendering was no like me. The time I was living through ought to be spent on all of the three main exams that I had to give within a space of two months. My future relied heavily on them.

But here I was, my belly swelling to the point that I couldn't eat anymore. Seeing my slim waist, which was one of the things that reassured me, and I loved about myself, growing bigger like a nine months pregnant woman depressed me like a serious patient. My sister took me to a doctor immediately, who was the only hope at that point. We weren't going to rely on voodoo ways. After getting to the hospital, my stomach was scanned. The doctor reported that

I had a considerable amount of fluids in there, and they were trapped. They weren't passing out. The only first aid help was to take all the fluids out and send a few fluids samples to the central Rwandan laboratory for testing. It was scary to hear that, for I know it was after such reports and laboratory testing that you find out something serious is wrong with you.

I was very desperate, and I could barely stand. The doctor spoke to my sister, telling her that she has to wait as they take the fluids out of my stomach. As I lay on one of those hospital beds in the surgery room, I couldn't help feeling terrified. I almost thought that I was going to pass away, that it was the end of my life since even the doctor did not know what I was suffering from.

The pain was just too much. My 55-year old doctor brought syringes, and I asked him if he is going to use anesthesia, and he said no. I started crying right away. At the end of the day, the doctor knew better. He knew what he had to do, so with the help of big needles, he connected the syringes to my belly and sucked out the liquid. I was watching it, my neck propped up. I was conscious of everything that was happening, inside and out, and God was it painful. After ten minutes of extracting fluids from my stomach, the doctor realized that he had not brought enough syringes. He fell short and had to leave me in the room to go and bring more from upstairs. The fragile me, I was left trembling on the bed with fluids coming out of my stomach. It was ugly. The image of myself at that moment will always be stuck in my head forever. I was feeling so helpless, almost lost hope for life. At that point, I wasn't feeling the pain anymore, nor did I think about the future. I just wanted to know at least what I was suffering from.

Two hours passed in the surgery room. The surgery was successfully completed, and my belly hole sealed. They called my sister to come and pick me up. I was released and took some of my fluids samples with me that we were supposed to take to the main national laboratory to get tested. I couldn't walk properly but was at least pleased that my belly swelling had reduced. It then looked like I had a significant injury on my belly and had to bend a little bit and waddle to complete my steps. My sister took the fluid samples to the laboratory. Luckily and gratefully, they did not find any disease. They only prescribed me painkillers.

Yet, my situation did not improve, and my mom decided, yet again, to take me to traditional doctors instead. She adamantly concluded that I had been poisoned. At her invitation, one of my mom's favorite pastors came home to pray for me. I, a girl of 18, was at the point where I couldn't even carry myself to the bathroom. I couldn't eat anything, and I was all drained and out of energy. My mom would sleep with me at night. I, on the other hand, could barely sleep.

The pain kept me up, and finding a good sleeping position was very difficult. My mom kept a small bucket at my side in which I would throw up. There was another bucket that I would use if I wanted to pee or poop. I felt like an ancient person, experiencing ills of extreme old age. I was dying in everyone's eyes, including mine.

You can imagine how difficult it must have been for my mother to even look at me when I was going through that horrendous illness. Her treatment of me was yet so devoted and courageous. That was one of the moments when I again realized how amazing mothers are. I was an adult, but at the moment, I need to be cared for just like a toddler since I couldn't do anything by myself. The needs ranged from eating to taking showers, and all of these things my mom was doing for me. I felt a special kind of pleasure and honor in that, if I may be honest. I had the opportunity to see my mom take care of me like a child in adult form. She did everything with so much love, empathy, and dedication, handled me with so much caution, just like she did when I was a toddler. It was a nostalgic time, and yes, while sweet to witness, felt heartbreaking at one point too.

I felt so undeserving. I mean, I appreciated everything my mom was doing for me, but remember I had made a promise to myself that I will one day make her happy and proud? That I would be the source of her relief and ease. That was the only way I could try to comfort myself. There was, in truth, no way I could simply do anything that would express how grateful I am for that woman.

No price in this human world would pay for even a third of what she did for me. I understand that everything she did. She was supposed to do it because she was my mother. She gave birth to me, and I came out of her like I was a part of her. And she ever loved me in that fashion. However, I was watching her do it yet again as an aged woman for an 18-year-old girl left a charring mark on my heart. I could read the worries, desperation, and frustrations on my mom's face upon finding me in that paralyzed condition, but she had the strength to try to remove her fears and keep a calm face when she looked at me. To tell you the truth, she sometimes did cry. She would bend her head, cover her face, and I would watch her shoulders shake violently, and moist drops would fall on my feet in spite of her covering her face with both hands. I was not even crying anymore, for I had passed that stage. My brain had blocked my emotions. I was not feeling anything at all.

My mom brought five pastors to pray for me, but nothing at all that they did worked. One of her friends recommended her this woman who lived two hours from my house. She was a catholic and a healer. She was said to pray for people's diseases, and through prayers, God used to tell her the medicine for every illness. This healer was said to be genuine, which reassured me all the more when I discovered that she did not charge anything for her services. They were absolutely free. The woman was said to be so well-known that many people and patients would come to her from other countries just for the medication. She was considered influential and held a saintly position in her village.

So we decided to go there right away and visit her. It must have been around 5 PM when my mom was told about that woman, and we went right away at 6 PM. Think about it. I honestly had slim hopes for survival. I thought I would die along the way, but we made it by the Grace of God. I met the woman. She had the typical shabby look about her. She heard my case and prayed for me for about 30 minutes.

My mom was praying along with her, as well. We sang some catholic songs together, and after everything was over, she too passed the verdict that I had been poisoned. She told me those people who had poisoned me wanted to take away my life.

To this day, I do not know who those people were. This was the reason that the doctor did not know of my illness either and couldn't decipher the name or cause, let alone the cure. I was shocked since I didn't remember having any enemies. I minded my business too much for that. But honestly speaking, I didn't know if she was right or wrong, yet I was so desperate to hear something about my condition. So again, I believed in the superstitious diagnosis and remedy.

She then gave me two bottles of liquids. One contained boiled water mixed with herbal and plant medicines and was filtered. I tasted it, and it was like water from the steamed green tea leaves. I was supposed to take a sip of each bottle every morning and every night before going to bed. Needless to say, I followed her instructions religiously. Surprisingly to say, I started getting better in three days.

My mother was as delighted as she was relieved. She had told my mom that we could come to her for more anytime. Discovering its curing qualities, I drank the medicine with so much passion. I wanted to get batter as soon as possible, and I could barely care that it tasted extremely bitter, but eventually, I couldn't even feel it. It was doing its job, and so it became, in fact, my favorite drink during those days.

One week later, I was feeling way better, and I had gained some strength, so I discussed with my mom the possibilities of returning to school. But you can guess what my mom would have said, a big definite no. Now the swell of my belly gone, I realized I had lost too much weight. It was true; I needed to be cared for before I could get back to school on my own. So I didn't rebel with my mother or anything like it. She had cared for me so diligently. The least I could do was listen to her to repay her efforts. Like that, I kept getting better and better every day. My mom was making me the most nutritious and delicious food I have tasted. They had unique ingredients in them, my mom's relief and happiness, and gratitude for my recovery. I don't know who told her that I don't have enough blood, and as a result, she was making me a homemade beetroots juice every day.

My diet also included fish, legumes, and other nutritious vegetables. My best friend, Rose, was also around. She would bring me this fantastic and fancy fish puree and make a bowl of homemade soup for me. It seemed like I was making up for all those early illness days when I couldn't pass any food down my throat.

I was grateful for Rose too. We both had grown up and become physically distant, yet she cared for me so profoundly. She would hang out with me the whole time I was at home. She would also somehow find ways to make little jokes, which made me feel a bit better. This applied for times even when I had gone numb and couldn't feel anything. In that sense, she became like a blessing to me. A few more days passed. My mom went back to the woman who gave me medicine to bring more bottles for me to take to school. Carrying them with me, I finally went back to school. It felt like a miracle to my mother, who had seen me throughout my sickness, and to me. It strangely reaffirmed some of my faith in good witch doctors. But ultimately, we thanked God for all the healing that came from him. When I arrived at school, I had lost almost 30 pounds in two weeks. I looked slender and tiny, and it was conspicuous.

Everyone kept inquiring about what happened to me. One after another, I would meet this peer or that, and the way they would eye me would give it all away. They were curious. What had happened to me? I did not have words to explain that. I truly lacked an answer myself, given the mysterious quality of the illness. So I subscribed to telling everyone that I just had a stomach-ache and that I lost appetite completely, the consequence of which was what they were seeing.

They were satisfied, and so was I.

Then came the challenge of gaining weight. For that, I tried to eat as much as I could every day. I was determined to bring my weight back to where it was in a matter of a few days. I dedicated to eating for my own health, and the delectable food at Gashora became like unhindered treats for me. I didn't focus much on how behind I was with the school and study schedule. I was simply grateful that I didn't pass away from life in that horrible state. That was enough reason for me to be happy. But then, of course, I could be happier, which was why I was gaining weight again. I had my first SAT exam three weeks after my return to school. It went reasonably well, but I did not get the minimum score requirement for most schools. I did not go too hard on myself, for that given how the ailment had been a reasonable impediment. I had to retake the SAT exam then, so I prepared for that.

A few weeks after, I took my TOEFL exam, and I supposedly did well since I got 80 out of 120. It was the minimum score requirement for the schools I was applying for, and since it was costly to take TOEFL, I decided not to repeat it. My scores were acceptable among most schools, so I didn't sweat it much. Both exams, TOEFL and SAT were paid for by my scholarship.

Time went by so quickly. Months of further preparation later, I finally gave my national exam. It was going to be the last exam from high school, the one that determines your destiny for life ahead. I had studied and prayed hard for myself. Furthermore, my class would hold a brief prayer every Wednesday night, and I would attend it each time. We would meet at the dorm and sing worship and praise songs. Believe me, when I say, the national exams are like the approaching end of the world. They make every student spiritual out of fear. It is the most feared exam amongst all. Everyone became a firm believer owing to the national exams. Nobody missed church for the few weeks before the grand test took place.

For the sake of solidarity and support, our teachers started joining as well. We had a small meeting with our school faculty members the night before the exam took place. They wanted to wish us good luck and talked about positive things to distract us from the fear that was in everyone's eyes. We needed a calm mind with a meditative concentration the next day.

Surprisingly, the faculty members themselves looked quite frightened and nervous. It mattered to them, for they had invested a great deal in us. Add to that; there was our school's reputation on the line. With trembling voices, they assured us. It was one of those moments where everyone was cold and sickly looking. Our school was one of the exam sites, and students from other schools would come and live with us for the next seven days of the national examination. The exam supervisors were policemen. I know police officers. This might be one of the things that only happen in Rwanda. The policemen invigilators made the exam scarier because cheating or attempting to cheat meant going to jail. This was made clear to us before the exam. The policemen and soldiers were streaming in and stationed all around my school the night before the national exam.

Looking at them, holding big guns with their stern faces and jaw set made me even more nervous. It was a bewildering case. The invigilators made us more nervous than the exam, and we feared for our destiny. I prayed internally that I don't get sick due to taking too much stress and pressure. I poured all of my concentration on how amazing my life will be in just seven days after all the national exams would be over.

That gave me the motivation and the courage to study harder. It is a trick that any of us can apply. We get so invested and engrossed in a present moment being hectic that we forget it will pass. Knowing that there is something good that I'm looking forward to giving me a kick, I needed to devour the dragon that hovered before me in the present.

Before I get to talking more about what happened inside the examination hall, let me tell you one more thing. A weekend before the exam, families were allowed to visit their children. All of our household members came and wished us good luck. I never expected my family to visit, given how distant it is, as well as difficult to access. It was incredibly surprising for me, thus, when my sister and Rose visited me. I was invigorated upon seeing them and finding someone close who had my back in person helped me study harder.

I wanted to make them proud, and I was sure it would be just the compensation for their sweet act of visiting me. My sister and Rose brought me different snacks and good luck cards. I was brimming with motivation due to their presence, and I couldn't wait for the exams to be over. What we did was we made plans of things we will do right after my exams.

Guess what, that injected further strong willpower in me to study. They hugged me tightly, patted my back, and had all the good wishes for me on their lips and faces before they left. It was the most loving thing they could do and was just what I needed at that moment. I had gotten it. On the day of the national exam, I was ready. I had slept for 8 hours, and I did not join the morning preps that everyone else indulged in. I wanted nothing to stress me out. I was at complete peace. I walked away from stressed-out students, and those last-minute-preparation students whom I knew for sure would be speaking out loud in the school what they memorized. Our school principal hugged every one of us before we entered the exam room. He looked very nervous than most of us but hid it behind his smiles. My mom had been making some calls throughout the week to wish me good luck. She would tell me that God is going to be there for me like he has always been.

There is a general rule I have observed. Once you manage to go through the first day of the exam successfully, the rest go by so swiftly. It was like a blink of an eye, and we had finally finished all the national exams on the 7th day. The next day, we had a huge celebration afterward. It was grand. We celebrated by throwing books and papers in the air as we made moves through the music rhythm. But there was a sadness to it too, of course. That day marked the end of us being together at the same time as a class of 90 students. We had built a strong relationship between each one of us despite the competition, but that realization we had pushed and had kept pushing until the very last moment. Ultimately, the moment came when all the dance moves slowed to sways and flutters, and all the hands went down to land to the hips gently. It was that moment that everyone was filled with emotions. It was over, we thought. The four yours of our lives, we had passed them through. Like an automatic memory reel, all of our four years played. We thought about the friendships and the most wonderful memories. But we had to say goodbye then.

I knew that I was going to see Giella even after school since she was my best friend, but I didn't know about others. So I hugged them, hard, like it was the last time. The hands of the clock may race, and we may meet along our journeys somewhere, but until then, that was the only moment I knew.

After parting ways, I kept wondering what was next for me as I waited for the national exam results. I had plans to stick around in Kigali since I had to have access to the internet and computers. My college applications were still due. I had to finish all of them for the two schools that the university advisors had told me to apply to Michigan State University and Arizona State University. Staying in Kigali also meant that I was going to be in someone else's house.

Of course, the school had ended, and I needed a place to stay. I thought about my uncle's place where my sister lived, but I was concerned about both of us being in my uncle's house. We may be a burden on them, but they didn't care about that. I was also concerned about my uncle's wife expecting me to act like my sister by waking up very early in the morning to do house chores.

I thought she would probably call me every time she needed something, which was not a big deal for me, given I was indebted to her for letting me stay. She, however, had a bad habit of sending people to bring her stuff. She didn't care if you have to go somewhere far to fetch it. As long as you get her what she wants, she's satisfied.

One day I remember she asked me to go and buy her favorite brand of milk. I thought it would be somewhere very close, but no. She wanted me to venture to the supermarket downtown, which was 40 minutes away. To make things worse, it was almost 8 PM at that time, with no car or bus to take me there. I had to take a motorcycle, and when I returned, she asked me to go back again. And then again. And one more time for something else she had forgotten. I had gone back to the store three more times. You may think there's nothing worse than this, but nope. That was not the first time she subjected us to this treatment. It was a regular part of our routine. I thought about it, and so, decided to stay with my godmother instead, who lived in Kigali. I had no money other than less than $10, which too my sister had given me the last time she visited me at school. I had to carefully utilize that money, for I had to travel almost every day, back and forth, to meet the person who was editing my college essays.

I would wake up very early in the morning and walk on my way to the library, which was an hour and a half away. I would take a bus on my way back for it saved me some money. It took me three weeks to complete my application forms and give a retake for the SAT. When I had finally submitted my application, I started wondering what will be my alternative plan if I don't get into the universities I applied to. I have heard my university advisor talking about this organization called '*Open a Door.*' It used to help selected young women to apply for American universities by providing them with SAT and TOEFL instructors, paying for their tests, and helping them with the application process. The organization would also find you American mentors, who would be like your American host parents when you make it to the USA. The only problem with *Open a Door* was that you had to take a gap year before going to college. I quickly applied to the organization, but I didn't know that I could or would get in. Like all tests in my life, it was very competitive. They were going to take only five to seven women in the country.

Following the application, I was invited for the first round of interviews and the second round of interviews. Finally, I got admitted after the third interview. It may not come as a surprise to you, given how you must read about all my successes. I was delighted, for it was a privilege to be selected for the organization.

The director of the program suggested that I take the SAT and TOEFL classes with others and retake the tests to improve my scores. It was totally fine with me since the problem was paying for all costs associated with those tests, and they were taking care of it. As I was taking the SAT and TOEFL with others, I also had to come up with another plan just in case everything else doesn't work out. I didn't want to take a gap year, so I decided to also apply to Africa Leadership University located in Mauritius. It was giving out full scholarship to outstanding African students from economically disadvantaged families. There is a pattern you are detecting here. Yes, my target was toward full scholarships because that was the only way for me to acquire higher education. My mom had made it clear – as if she needed to – that she can't afford to pay for college. And so, I went ahead and applied to my third university.

After I was done with that, something still didn't feel right. I wasn't satisfied with all I have done. I still wanted a plan D. When I reflect on it now, the truth is that I was scared of the future, and I wanted to be successful no matter what. Every time I thought about what I would do if everything goes wrong, I would quickly find another plan. I had so much fear of uncertainties, and I was also determined to be successful no matter what it took.

My future was in my hands. I knew full well that my mom had done her part by offering me a high school education. She had raised me to the point I was, had gotten me out of the dangerous lifestyle of Congo. It was now my turn to be on my own and navigate life like an adult I was growing to be. And I was going to show that to them as a surprise.

My family didn't know anything about what I was doing. Nobody knew about my application journey or the tests that I had to take. It was a secret known only to me that I was a member of *Open a Door*. I kept everything to myself. One reason was that a part of me wanted to surprise them with the results of all I had been working on. I wanted my success to speak to them rather than just telling them what I was currently working on. The second reason was that I didn't want my mom to have extra hopes.

If I would have told her what I was doing and then, God forbid, couldn't have made it… then what? I didn't want anyone to sympathize with me if I don't get admissions. It was easier to deal with disappointments and failures when only I was involved. When no one knows about your stumbles but you, you don't get any laughs.

These were my reasons not to involve my family in what I was doing. I also felt like it will give them a false hope, which can lead to further disappointment. I always love to announce the results of completed tasks than announcing about my efforts. I proceeded with my plan D, which was applying for the Rwandan-based branch of Kepler University. As I have mentioned, it was also giving out full scholarships, and it was easier to apply there since I had all the application materials ready. After that, my final plan was to apply for Rwandan universities, as in the local ones. I put in my applications for all these categories, and after that, my heart was at peace. It knew that I did my level best and have exhausted all of my options. I knew that one way or the other, I will definitely get a scholarship. What was the probability of not getting one out of four of my options, after all? 20 percent.

Its contender was 80 percent, and that probability gave me so much peace. I continued to take the SAT and TOEFL classes together with other students and worked diligently to do better than the last times. I was delighted and proud of all I have done, and I was ready to accept whatever comes from it. It would be by no means wrong to say that I was optimistic about what was coming ahead.

The national exam results were released in early February, and I made everyone proud upon scoring 64 out of 73 in the exams. I was over the moon and extremely happy for it was among the best results. Not a single person in my family had ever received such handsome grades. I deserved all the pats on my back, including one I would give to my self. However, I knew I needed to deal with humbleness and gratitude, too, for where had I been if not for all the prayers and good wishes my elders, peers, and most especially my family made for me? Quite soon, what must have been early March, I found myself sitting in my SAT preparation classroom, and my phone suddenly buzzed. I fished it out to find an email, a congratulation email from Arizona State University.

They had announced my name among their MasterCard scholarship winners. I was one of them, the thought alone sent raptures scurrying all over me. I WAS ONE OF THE FEW WHO GOT A FULL SCHOLARSHIP TO ATTEND ARIZONA STATE UNIVERSITY. How could I not scream and shout out loud at that news? Like pfft, come on. That is just what I did.

I caused a jolt amongst all the students when I screamed. They all looked at me with a *"What is going on here,"* look in their eyes. What did I do as a result? I screamed even louder, louder and louder I went, thinking how one email could change your world and life, flip it upside down to a smile from a frown.

I don't know how I came to recover from that delight. All I remember is senselessness due to extreme joy. Oh, and I also remember thinking to myself that I hoped it was not a dream. I kept telling myself that. And out of my class, I went and right away called my mom with a heart spinning like a tornado. I was going to the US. I was going to one of the very excellent universities there were.

And so I told my mom, I spilled my guts out, no idea in what order and there was so much frenzy. My mother was shocked out of her head, of course. It was a maddening surprise for her because she did not even know that I had applied for this scholarship. And so, we both were screaming on the phone. Haha, God, what a moment that was. I still count it as one of the best ones in my life.

My mind was running wild, and my heart was going frantic. I wanted to celebrate this achievement so badly. Somehow my brain did the thinking. I knew just how I was going to celebrate it. I had always loved mangoes and apples with all the earnestness in the world. So, though it may sound plain to you, I decided to buy the best mangoes and apples and eat them for lunch. It happened to become one of the best meals for me. I naturally loved fruits, not that I don't any longer; it's just that some fruits like apples were only for the rich people in Rwanda. They were too expensive. So it turned out to be an adequate treat from me to me. After that, I dashed across and stood before a mirror, looking at myself and smile wild like a madwoman. My face was full of smiles, and I just couldn't help feeling how wonderful life was. I was going to America, a girl from the woods of Congo, going to America for my higher studies.

One week later, Michigan State University announced its winners as well. Surprise, surprise, I was one of them too. My world was on mad wheels. Things were working out more than perfect for me. I celebrated that as well, but let's spare you the details about that. You've borne too much exuberance already, dear readers.

I am coming back to the point. So, after that getting that acceptance too, I had to choose which university I wanted to attend between Michigan State and Arizona State University. I was weighing my decision when I remembered that I had a friend from my high school at Michigan State University. And then it snows in Michigan, which I was curious to experience, so I ended up choosing Michigan State University. Ta-da!

Open a Door organization asked me if I wanted to stay as an organizational member with them, and I said yes. They then found me mentors in the USA, four amazing women who became a huge part of my life later on. Among these crazy progressions, I didn't lose grip on the fact that my life was changing; that this was it, the grand ascension. My dreams were slowly becoming real, and I just felt so grateful for everything. I wanted to share my happiness with the whole world.

As you have gotten the hint, I am a private person. I called my mom and asked her and my sister to keep everything confidential. This way, only my siblings and my parents knew about my offer – or should I say offers. No one else in my family had an inkling of an idea. I liked it like that.

I then started dreaming and imagining my life in the USA. I started fantasizing about how the USA looks like and the kind of lifestyle that I was soon going to be a part of. I imagined the blue sky on a sunny day, wearing my perfect outfit and walking around in a place that looked like San Francisco or New York in my imagination. I imagined arriving at Michigan State University and being welcomed with so much love from my white friends. I wondered how it would all feel like to have a heartwarming reception such as that, as I had never been in a room dominated by white people. I could, in every sense, only imagine it. Given how wild my imagination runs, I also imagined meeting this handsome white guy on campus. In my imagination, he asked me out, and I agreed like a lady. He then came in fancy suits to pick me up on our first date. I imagined myself wearing a long beautiful gown looking like Cinderella going on my first date.

I imagined being happy and always remembering my family in those times, sharing with them every potential gladdening news. I succeeded and graduated summa cum laude from my university and got hired for a fantastic job, which helped me grow, and every day was a new fun challenge. After my job, I was going to buy my family a house, probably just a few months after.

And of course, my fantasies did not end just there. I imagined taking long walks at the most beautiful beaches I have seen in movies with exquisite sunsets. I was wearing a bikini on my perfect trim and toned body. I also imagined being able to eat as much meat as I can – without putting on much weight and chicken and fish diets to be more specific.

We used to eat fish only once a year in my family, and that was at Christmas. The meat was relatively common, a once in a week diet. Whenever my mom would cook meat, everyone would get two pieces each. Those two pieces of meat, I ate them with all the relishing. I wanted to stop eating it in a pinchpenny way. I wanted to gobble up as much and as I wanted when it comes to fish and chicken.

Furthermore, among my meals, I imagined eating apples every day, unlike at home. Would you believe, some of my extended family had never tasted apples due to how expensive they are! Lastly, apart from meals, I imagined being taken for shopping by my wealthy American friends. In a nutshell, I simply imagined an easy and fun life. These were my set expectations from the USA.

I started applying for my passports and Visa, and my departure was slowly arriving – see what I did there? The mentors that I was given by Open a Door organization were very kind to me, and they kept sending me the instructions for my first flight. Yeap, I was going to fly on the airplane for the first time. Remember I told you about the mentor women? Well, I loved them all with all my heart. One of them acted like a mother to me. How? She worried at every step of mine, just like a mother, asking for constant updates, and freaking out when there didn't come any. She sent me two-paged printed instructions about my first flight so that I would get familiar and cozy about the whole process. It was so endearing not to feel judged for being a first-time flyer at such an age.

I distinctly remember one of our conversations well before the flight. She had called me on my phone to make sure everything was going well. She was like, *"Josine, get to the airport three hours before your flight, your seat will be the window seat... Make sure to run to your next gate when you land to Amsterdam... don't miss your next flight. Say okay, come on."*

One week before my departure, I started panicking and felt a lot of fear in my heart and stomach. I had even lost my appetite, though it wasn't fractionally as bad as that belly swelling thing, so don't worry. It mainly related to the feeling of flying and leaving my family behind. That was truly terrifying. So yes, I had been staying with my immediate family at this time. I had by then informed my close friends about the admission, and everyone was just reminding me and turning me emotional about the fact that I would be leaving them soon. I tried to stay calm, but with two days left until my departure, I couldn't for the life of me keep it in. Things changed. My eyes started to water by themselves at times, and the blues overtook me. As I started saying goodbye to some of my relatives, the fear was getting out of my hands. It deepened and deepened until it felt like I had a heart attack. No longer was I excited about the whole thing anymore.

Maybe some part in me was, but at that particular point, it was buried quite deep. And so I was not excited anymore about going. I was emotional, throughout the time I was packing and making final arrangements, there was this sense of loss, of leaving from my roots and origins. One day before the flight, Rose came to our house and spent the entire day with me. I had everything sorted and together in the material sense, but my heart and mind were other stories.

I had to go to the school before the fall semester started upon my mentors' request. They wanted us to have time together, get a proper introduction and orientation, and wanted to show me around the city and the school before the semester started. I heard that there was another girl from my high school who had gotten accepted into Michigan State

University. That was a curious and exciting scenario, but unfortunately, we had different flights because I departed one week early. I had to fly all alone from Kigali to Lansing. The thought alone was terrifying. The night before my flight, my whole family – extended included – was there with me. They traveled along to spent a night with me in Kigali, closer to the international airport. It was a warm experience, something that made me celebrate my solidarity. My mom got me a small gift, which was an art portrait with the African continent on it. A 'Thank you' was printed on it, and I immediately knew what it meant. She wanted me never to forget them, to continually think about home and my roots.

As soon as I saw the present, I burst out crying. Imagine a flood inside you gushing out in waves. That's what it was like. I just couldn't hold myself together at that moment. In fact, holding myself together was the last thing on my mind. I hugged her tight, for I don't even know how long.

After my last dinner with them, my sister startled the life out of me when she brought a bottle of champagne out. It was a farewell party they had surprised me with, and I received gifts from everyone. We celebrated until it was late night by when I had no energy remaining in me. The clocks were ticking. The final departure was approaching, and my heart was rising by the tick up till the base of my throat. How was I going to leave them? Home is where the heart is, they say. That group, that marvelous group of people whom I had learned so much from, especially my immediate family, they had the whole of my heart. And of course, their teaching sessions were not going to end there.

That's when the time for advice came. It started with my uncle, who talked for almost an hour, telling me how to conduct and represent my family and my country overseas. He told me to avoid 'temptation' and always to remember my purpose for the travels, why I am in the states in the first place. It was to build a prosperous future for myself, he said. He asked me never to change who I am at my roots and under my skin.

I was not to try to conform to the American culture. He added that I should keep my Rwandan culture preserved in me and should acknowledge that I am a Rwandese wherever I go. After his long speech, my best friend followed. She was very emotional and at a loss for words. She would begin and fumble, and so the only thing she said and stopped at was that she would deeply miss me. Once she was done, we hugged each other. My sister followed with another emotional speech, and I was just an emotion slob leaking uncontrollable tears by that time. I couldn't hold myself; I was crying as much as I had never cried before. I was crying oceans. And the best part was that they let me. These were the last moments, and they were all mine. Mine. Nobody was going to restrict me from making and absorbing my memories in the way I wanted.

My uncle ended the lush and soppy party by giving me $50. It was kept in an envelope, and that was supposed to be the only money I would carry and was going to have when I left Rwanda for the States. Even though so much had passed, it felt as if the night had gone by too fast. I don't think I slept at all. I was with all of my girls on the same bed that night.

The last night with them. Another beautiful and memorable moment. It made me feel safe, or should I say it gave me an illusion of safe while I was still worried and scared about leaving. Finally, on the day of my first flight, the flight away from Rwanda came. I was petrified and sick because of the fear in my heart. So drained, I had lost all energy and felt the weight of the world on my shoulders. It was, in fact, as if I was leaving my world, my little haven I had made in the 19 years of my life. I was crestfallen, empty-stomached because I couldn't eat anything and aimless as to what to focus on in those final moments of being in my homeland. I felt empty, just like I was going to die. I know optimism slays and all. I know that I had a beautiful life ahead in a metropolitan. It was going to be blissful and full of adventures. I knew all of that. Nevertheless, it was a sign of my love and devotion to be engrossed in the present moment.

Hours were moving by quickly, and my flight was at 8 PM. I had to depart well before that, for I had to be at the airport by 5 PM per my mentors' instructions. And guess what? My mother wanted me to be there by 4 PM just in case. It was a case of only in case upon a just in case, for even my mentors had mentioned three hours before just in case.

Other friends of mine around the town came to our house to say goodbye that night. Our house was full as if there was a wedding or a party ongoing. So remember, my uncle had given me $50? My sister made sure to take all other money that I had accumulated except the $50. She was like, *"you don't need money, you are going to the USA, and you will get a lot more of it. So give me that."* I was in such a fuzzy mind state that I wasn't even thinking properly, and I gave her everything she asked for, including some of my favorite clothes. It later felt like someone took advantage of me while I was drunk or something, for in that moment, I complied to her every wish. She had gone through all of my things and had picked out whatever she wanted.

The time to go to the airport finally came. Reaching at four meant leaving at three, and that's what we did. We took a van in the dark of the night to take us there at the airport. So many people came to say goodbye to me, even people who barely knew me. These included people such as my mom's friends, but familiar ones, too, like my godmother, my sister's friends, my uncles, and so on.

I was crying in the van all the way to the airport, and I didn't even want to go anymore. It was a sentimental frame of mind I was in, and it felt excruciating to say goodbye to my city, my country, my family. I wasn't thinking about my future, and my career ahead, the ambitions that were going to benefit the same family through me. I just did not want to leave. I had been away from my family, like at Gashora, and even after graduating, something felt a little more permanent than before that flight. I cried and ended up screaming when it was my time to go. I tried to resist entering the airport gate but the airport security guide had to take me inside by force. That was the point beyond which my family could not enter, and that was where my sense returned to me. I accepted and acknowledged the situation and waved at my family until we lost sight of one another.

After entering the airport, I stumbled upon my high school principal. He was also flying abroad to Amsterdam, and it felt good to have found someone to fly with. I was still sniffling and crying. The kind man bought me a box of juice, and he assured me that everything would be fine. He congratulated me on my success and told me that I would do well at Michigan State University.

Sitting inside the airport at gate eight, waiting for my flight, I wiped away all of my tears and looked around. I was all alone with strangers, and I realized most starkly that I was now on my own. I had to comfort myself and remind myself how much I wanted this moment and how much I wanted to go abroad. I decided to leave my worries behind and look forward to the new life that was waiting for me. I told myself that I was going to be just fine and successful.

I looked down at my pocket. I only had $50, which was the single highest amount of money I had owned in my 19 years of living. I then took a deep breath and allowed my new adventure to begin. It was my first time to be inside the airport, so I focused my attention on absorbing this first time experience. I discovered the airport escalators were just too terrifying.

I tried to watch what other people were doing, but suddenly it all morphed to become something too scary. I thought I was falling down vertigo. On the escalators, I hated the end and the beginning of those mechanical stairs. I would try to stretch my feet so as to make a smooth transition from escalators to standard airport tiles, but I would nearly break my feet.

Somehow, as if losing time, I found myself inside the airplane. As I was waiting for the plane to take off, I peered down the window to look at my beautiful country. I wished I could see my family just one more time right then. But I decided to say goodbye for the last time. As the plane flew above Kigali city, I kept saying *"Goodbye"* to everyone by mentioning their names. Friends and family and everyone whom I remembered to have curated and contributed to my experience of life in Rwanda. I knew this flight was going to change my life forever, but for the best. I kept looking outside the window until I lost sight of my country. All I could see were some dots of lights here and there. But that quote crossed my mind. Don't cry because it's over. Smile because it happened. I welcomed my new life with a smile, and in my heart, I made a small prayer. I asked God to protect me and be with me on the new journey that I had just started, all alone.

I was aware that I was alone and on my own, and it was not the first time, but still, it kind of was. It was my first time alone, being in a completely unfamiliar place. And it was hitting me so hard. I couldn't call my mom or my sister to help me with anything. I left my friends behind, and I had no friends where I was going. All the people I knew were three mentors, who were nearly strangers to me, whom I couldn't entirely be sure about by that time.

All of that deeply hurt me inside, but I smiled on and decided to be healthy. It was the only option I had anyway, and I spoke out a few affirmation statements that everything was going to be okay. I said out loud that I will make new good friends and that I will be successful. I was determined to navigate my life fearlessly. That was the last thing I remember saying, and then I soon fell asleep. I woke up two hours later when the flight attendant was serving dinner. I couldn't believe how hungry I was and simultaneously excited for my first plane meal. They served us chicken and some rice, cheese, salads, and a loaf of bread on the side with mango juice. (Yes, Mango juice). The food was delicious. I savored every bite and every sip of the meal.

My new life was starting to feel good with my stomach full. The flight from Kigali to Amsterdam lasted eight hours, and I was getting too tired, only thinking that I had another eight hours flight to make through. The journey was too long and tiring, but ultimately, we landed in Amsterdam. Looking at the beautiful Netherlands weather from outside my window, I was wondering what the US will be like if Amsterdam itself appeared so unreal.

I had my instructions with me that my mentor had given, and following that, I rushed to find the gate number for my next flight. My school principal was with me there as a guide. We had taken separate flights then from Amsterdam to the USA. Amsterdam airport was huge, and my gate number there had changed at the last minute. In light of that,

I had to walk for thirty minutes to get to my next gate number. I was exhausted and famished, but I was too reluctant to spend any of the $50 I had with me. It accounted for my entire wealth at the time, and I wanted to save it for a rainy day or moment.

Enduring hunger and thirst had been a long-time habit, so I was hoping I was going to manage that. I just didn't know what to expect after I got to the USA and what might require me to spend my money.

Life in USA and Michigan State University

My next flight was from Amsterdam to Minneapolis. It took place, and I landed on my first ever USA airport. The flight again took eight hours, and I tried to sleep a little bit. In the end, I couldn't. I was very uncomfortable in the plane but very excited to get to Minneapolis. The USA was a dream, my dream, and I desperately wanted to see what it looked like.

I was watching the city from the plane window before we were going to land in Minneapolis. It looked amazing from afar. My mouth was frozen in a *"whoa"* as I looked at it. It made me wonder how the city would look like closer up. As I got out, however, I realized I was too tired to care about the city or anything else except my destination. The last flight I took was from Minneapolis to Lansing.

It was there that I was going to meet my mentors, and I couldn't wait for it. My mentors were regularly updating me, and I knew they had flown all the way from California to Michigan to see me. Arriving at Lansing airport, I saw this short, skinny, strong, and funny woman with a great post written on *"Welcome Josine."* It was my mentor Mary, and looking at her, I felt relief wash over me. I had reached my new home. By Mary's side, there was Barabara, tall, skinny, with a severe face. When her eyes found mine, she instantly erupted with so much joy. I hugged both of them very tightly, and it felt lovely to meet them. Mary and Barbara were so lovely to me, continually inquiring if I was comfortable and wanted something to eat or drink. Exiting the airport, I found myself on American soil. I rode in their car and was stunned by the visuals I was seeing.

Lansing was like a place of eternal spring, infested with so many trees, a few houses, and you could hardly see any people outside. It was still nothing like I had imagined. I also noticed expensive-looking cars and very neat roadsides. The only thing close to my imagination the city contributed to was the soil, mud, and dust, which I did not find anywhere in the city. Everything was super clean.

I secretly hoped that we would soon get to a more urban, some New York kind of a place. As we kept driving, we moved away from the houses and came to a place called Castle Park. That's where we were supposed to spend a night and a week before I went off to school. Castle Park had beautiful nature scenes with foreign trees around that I did not know names of. I was, for the first time, the only black person around a place. Throughout the journey, I found myself looking outside to see if I could find another black person. I did not have any luck there. My mentors, and I soon had dinner, and the only thing I could remember of that moment was chicken. It was a real treat to enjoy. Mary introduced me to her parents, who were also staying at Castle Park for the summer. She introduced me to the jolly couple, and I felt so bad about feeling tired already of my third proper introduction. I was fully aware that it was just the beginning of it.

I had no cell phone, and there was no way to talk to my family. I borrowed their phone so that I could text my sister on Facebook that I had a safe journey. I had so many things that I wanted to tell everybody at home. About the journey, the sights, the city, my mentors.

In spite of the pleasant reception, I couldn't fully relate with them and neither openly talk to them. I was with two nice women, but I had just met them. Trust doesn't come all that easily to me. My first night in the USA was too long, and I couldn't sleep half of the night due to the time difference from where I was coming from. I was always talking to myself in the local language because there was no one else to understand it. I was also compelled to speak

English the whole time, which also limited my talking. One day later, there was a gathering at Castle Park where there was a lot of food and many older people. Mary wanted to introduce me to almost everybody. I found myself to be the only black girl around and so I was more noticeable in the way I stood out. I introduced myself to more than twenty people that night. The introduction entailed my name, my background, and the purpose of my visit.

Mary would add on that I'm the girl she was mentoring from Rwanda, who received a scholarship to attend Michigan State University, and this was my second day in America, it was my first time flying too, she told them. She would continue *saying, "I met Josine through Open a Door, an organization that helps women to apply to USA universities, and it matches them with American Mentors."*

I kept my smile on, but I was so exhausted from introducing myself and not to mention repeating myself due to my thick foreign accent. They could hardly comprehend what I was saying. Mary's relative would keep asking me where Rwanda is, for they knew nothing about it. Telling them, I was from Rwanda was making things a little hard for me because I had to go on and explain that Rwanda is a country located in East Africa. Then I came with a hack and decided to make my life easy by saying that I was from Africa. I also decided to concentrate on my food so that I don't have to talk too much. I would keep heading over to the food station, and there was this spicy looking meat there. I would keep adding some to my place, but when I tried them, they had sugar in them.

The chicken tasted sweet to me, so I stopped eating it. At the end of the gathering, I was so fed up with everything, tired and annoyed that nobody knew my country and that the food tasted nothing as it looked. I ended up getting an intense headache that night, and I wished I could escape somewhere alone to cry. I wished my sister was around or anyone else really back from home with whom I could talk to. But it should go without saying that I was grateful for being there.

The next morning we went to the nearby beach. I watched my mentors swim effortlessly, and since I didn't know how to swim, they tried to teach me, but I was too scared. So they kept swimming, and I stayed by the lake shores. I have always loved being at the beach and taking long walks along the sands, but the American beach that I had in my mind wasn't exactly the same as the small lake we went to. It seemed different from my expectations and imagination. Though I knew I had to hold on, and I was just struggling from the transition from one country to the next. The days were passing, and time to go to school was approaching, so my mentors took me shopping. We bought a lot of dorm room stuff, and I was the one picking everything. We went to this store that was new to me called Target, and I was overwhelmed by the variety of things on the shelves.

It was my first time being in that kind of a store where there was no interaction between the buyers and the sellers, where the concept of bargaining was nonexistent, where you paid the exact amount as mentioned on the product tag. Every single thing looked mighty expensive to me since I was converting the dollar into the local currency in my head.

There were so many choices to make, especially given that every single product had different varieties and brands of the same product. Now, thankfully I had a model to shortlist things not to be fazed by the paradox of choice. Red has always been my favorite color and I used that to help me pick what I wanted for my dorm room. I realized that I felt very excited to go to school. One more thing that motivated me was after I had seen the pictures of the Michigan State

University Campus. It was otherworldly. I had never seen any campus premises like that, and I couldn't wait to see and explore it all with my own eyes. The day finally came, and we packed everything up and zoomed away. I was so ready to be dropped at school. But given how nervous I was, I didn't know what to expect from the Michigan State University campus for myself.

As we were driving toward the MSU campus, I saw a big road sign indicating that we have entered the university premises. I initially thought that there would be a huge fence surrounding the campus, and we will probably have to pass through the campus gates. Instead, it was just connected roads that led to the campus with no fence or anything that indicated that it was a college campus.

Once inside, I feel the best way to describe it is that it looked like a small city. So we kept driving inside the MSU campus. I was very surprised by the beauty and the size of the campus. The campus looked vernal with all its green summer grasses, green trees all around, and super clean roads. Everything seemed so perfect, the grasses, the trees, the topiaries all immaculately trimmed. The buildings were all majestically constructed too. The campus was exceeding my expectations. I suddenly imploded with the happy and lucky feeling that I was going to be able to spend my next four years on that beautiful campus. I pictured myself jogging in the evenings and walking around from classes and appreciating the beauty of the school. My heart was filled with so much joy and awe at these imaginations.

It was a fifteen-minute drive to my dorm. Imagine fifteen minutes, and that too in a car! I couldn't believe a university would be this big to the extent where you have to drive for 15 minutes from one part of the campus to another. I couldn't help realizing how wildly my horizons were going to expand in the USA.

Arriving at my dorm, my mentor and I were given campus maps and room keys. My mentor, Barbara, helped me arrange my dorm room, and I did everything hurriedly. We then went to take a campus tour while taking pictures, of course, and I couldn't wait to send them to my sister. As part of the tour, we went to one of the nicest cafeterias at Michigan State University ate lunch there. Barbara advised me to eat especially more sushi, vegetables, and fruits. She wanted me to stay as healthy as I could. The time to say goodbye to her was soon approaching, and as our farewell, she gave me a plant, insisting that I needed to have life in my dorm room. She then hugged me very tightly and wished me all the best. After the hug, Barbara looked worried to leave me all alone there. I could see her eyes watering, and I was crying as well. But it was the end of our first journey as mentors and mentees. We had to say goodbye there.

I went back to my room with my map and later sat on my bed, just wondering what I was supposed to do. Everything seemed to be vast in this side of the world, and looking at all the vastness, I was reminded that I was all alone. I was both physically and emotionally alone, trying to figure out what to do in my room. There really was nothing left to do, given that I had already arranged my clothes. So I decided to pick up my map and take a walk.

I walked for thirty minutes on the campus, and on my way back, I couldn't distinguish which building was my dorm since most of them looked the same. And suddenly, I had no idea how to use the map. I couldn't help getting lost even more by trying to follow the map, which I later realized that I was using wrongly. I then asked one girl on the street the direction to South Wonders, which was my dorm name.

This was a tall white girl, and she replied to me, *"Walk toward the Shaw lane street and turn to birch road street. South Wonders will be on your left."* I didn't know what these streets addresses were or how I was supposed to identify a street name. Everything was so new to me. This mode of directions-giving was too complex for me.

When I had asked for directions, I expected her to direct me the African way, which is *"Keep walking, you will then see a big tree where there is a red brick building. Turn by that building toward the tennis court. There is usually a man who is always standing there in a red jacket. Your destination will be right by the tennis court."*

Given that, I was more confused after asking for directions. I started getting worried about walking back and forth. Trying not to walk too far, I finally saw another guy who was walking towards me. I then asked him for directions to my dorm. Fortunately, he was going right there and agreed to take me with him. And like that, I returned to my dorms. And ladies and gentlemen, that was my day one at Michigan State University! When I finally got to my room, I started googling how to use maps for directions. From then onwards, I did not want to get lost again.

This chaos did not change the fact that the university was very beautiful. Silly as it sounds, I would imagine all the romantic walks I could take there if only I could find a boyfriend as quickly as I had imagined before coming to the USA. As I walked around on campus, I would observe everyone I met, especially the cute boys. I kept a bold eye out for them. Among them, I really appreciated the beauty of every single one I met, even though they had not become my friends. I only hoped that I would have one of those cute boys soon for me soon.

One thing I kept realizing on the MSU campus was that people kept asking me if I had an event to attend since I was always overdressed. It was like I was a university student full of hopes and dreams before exams start kicking in. But in my head, I wasn't doing something out the ordinary. After all, students back home in Rwanda dress professionally for classes, and that was the image I had in my mind of a typical outlook of a college student in America too.

Hence, I was determined to act and look like one. I would put on my red lipstick every day with my colorful and sexy but sophisticated outfits. It made me feel good, despite having to answer the same question of whether I have an event to attend other than classes. On my third day of classes, I remember it was a beautiful sunny day, and I had decided to wear my favorite green high waist jeans with a grey crop top. The jeans hugged my hips so well that I secretly wanted to sleep with my own self. As I was walking towards my dorm, I was trying to take a selfie so that I could send it to my sister. To my lack of knowledge, this tall chocolate skinned boy walked by whom I would find was returning from basketball practice. *"Hi, sexy,"* I heard the voice say. Shocked but quickly recomposing, I said Hi back and embarrassed, tried to walk on faster.

The handsome man stood in my way and blocked it so that I couldn't take any further step without hitting him. He asked for my name. I said, *"Josine,"* and tried to walk past him, but he wouldn't let me. He kept walking too close to me until there was almost zero distance between us. I grew very frustrated and nervous because I had never had an experience such as that. He then asked for my number and clearly refused. I didn't want to give it to him, but then he held my hands, and I wanted to be far away from him, so I gave it to him. All I wanted then was to be away from him. I hoped he was going to let me go. But you wouldn't believe it… This time he brought his face close to my ears and whispered, *"Can I get a hug?"* My heart started beating so fast that very instant. I wanted to scream, but again my instincts were telling me that I might be overreacting. It may not be that serious in American culture. Yet, I did not want to give in. I remembered just then an old technique that I used to do to get away from someone by faking a phone call, so I faked one right there. With my trembling, frightened voice, I kept repeating on the phone that I will be there in a minute so that he would hear that I have an emergency and needed to leave.

And like that, he finally let go of my arm, and I ran as fast I could. What had just happened to me? I couldn't wrap my mind around the fact that I was in the middle of the road, and everyone kept walking past me while the basketball guy was harassing me. Minding their businesses, they just kept going on and on.

It may not be a serious deal to someone else, but for me, it was another reminder that I was alone and that nobody cared about whatever happens to me. I needed to protect myself, speak for myself, and fight for myself. One of the girls I shared this event with that day advised me to buy pepper spray. They told me that everyone seemed to have one except me. It was apparently a stock requirement. I still couldn't imagine a situation where I will have to use pepper spray, but again you can never be too safe considering the incident that just happened to me. I assumed it was a once in a blue moon case, yet, the probability wasn't zero.

I was told first-year students live the best life in college since they don't have that much to do in their first year. My advisor had added that we were in the honeymoon phase of college, so I should have as much fun as I could. On the other hand, there was me. I was emotionally drained and tired due to worrying about my GPA already, my family, and my future. For some reason, I kept worrying about what was next after college only in my first days as a freshman.

My scholarship required me to maintain a GPA of above 3.0; otherwise, I would lose my scholarship. I couldn't help worrying about making sure that I secured that number. This alone took away my peace every time I thought about it. It was such a conflicting state of mind. I was confident that I was going to do well in classes, but the fear of failure kept circulating in my veins. I had to remind myself that failure was not an option for me; I couldn't fail, and I wasn't going to fail. Since I was not too sure about how I was going to do in my first semester, that uncertainty drove me to think about plan B and plan C, just in case I lost my scholarship or failed some class. Throughout this while, I was in touch with my family. Most of those who had known me kept sending me text messages reminding me how lucky I was to be in the USA. They added that I shouldn't take anything for granted and live my life with reasonable pleasure.

These messages and the hope that people had in me added more weight to my worries, as always. I never wanted to disappoint anyone, and most of all, myself. My primary purpose has always been to be able to do the things that my dad would have done for my family if he was still alive. This included things such as building a house for my family.

This ensured that my siblings had a glorious future, and my mom all the happiness that I could afford. My mom had sacrificed everything to raise us, and I wanted to make her old days peaceful and enjoyable. I had to be successful no matter what to achieve all of the above. For this reason, failure has never been an option for me. Instead, if one plan doesn't work, I make sure to have another plan as an open option. At that point, I got a part-time job on campus.

My family was thrilled and were expecting me to send them money too. I myself couldn't wait to have my first stipend so that I could buy my mom something special. It has always been my dream to have enough money to send home, and I felt honored and humbled that it was made possible for me. I got my first stipend worth $250. It was the highest amount of money I had received in my twenty years of living. I was absolutely stunned and couldn't help thinking that I was rich now. I couldn't wait to share the happiness with my family.

I had a list of plans with my money, and one of them was buying my family a big screen TV and a carpet for home. I sent almost all of my stipend to cover for the TV and the carpet. And with the remaining money, I offered to pay school fees for my brothers since I was about to have a considerable amount of money each month.

As for what you might be wondering, no, I did not care much about what I wanted. And then again, my scholarship covered all of my accommodation costs too, which tends to be a vital issue for college students. So I only had to worry about toiletries, which did not cost me that much. It was easy to live with keeping my monthly expenses below $100. I did not eat out, especially in my first month, and neither did I take an Uber - which are another two fundamental expenses. I always preferred taking a bus to keep my expenses as low as possible. It was working for me just fine. It was in the second month that I had gotten a part-time job. My limited budget kept me away from partying and doing other activities that might involve overspending money. For me, every penny I got was a reminder of the terrible conditions my family was living in. I never let their thought overshadow my immediate gratification always carried the reminder of my family situation and my goals for them.

Away from the financials and back to my studies now. Keeping up with my classes got easier and easier as I started getting used to the USA education system. I was still struggling with lab reports and lab classes in general. It was largely because we had to work in teams most of the time, and I felt like I was neither considered nor noticed in any of my lab groups. Every time I tried to make a point or a suggestion to my lab partners, they kept on asking me to repeat myself due to my strong accent. Given the frequency with which that happened, I couldn't help feel offended sometimes.

Other times when I did end up successful in making a great suggestion, they always had to double-check it to make sure that what I said was correct. It was unbelievable for them. It is as if it was impossible that someone who didn't speak perfect English can make a correct point. That was another thing that made me feel undervalued and disrespected. It is very hard to feel motivated to ask questions in class, too, knowing that even the professor is probably not going to understand what you are trying to say.

Getting tired of repeating myself to them, I started to sit on the front row of my lecture rooms to make it easy for me to inquire. Despite that, the first time I tried to ask a question in my biology class, my professor asked me to repeat my question three times. On the fourth time, I told him that I found the answer.

From that day onwards, I never asked questions in class again. I preferred going to the professors during their office hours. That way, if they asked me to repeat my question, I wouldn't mind because it was only my professor, instead of the whole lecture room of two hundred plus students, and me. In this manner, every day for me had its own challenges. I felt more and more lost every day. I struggled at making new friends in this environment, which made me start questioning my social skills. The thing is that the problem was never me; it was just another adjustment that I needed to make. My academic advisor suggested me to join as many clubs as I could and try to attend as many events as possible. He said it would be a good way to make new friends and to meet new people. Attending events that I did not want to participate in it for the sake of making friends was very exhausting for me. I tried but eventually got tired of it.

Speaking of joining clubs, I tried to find clubs that instead might interest me. So, joining clubs for interest's sake rather than for friends. I joined the ballet dance club after the club president said that you don't necessarily need to have the experience to join. I had realized I would really enjoy dancing, which inspired me to go forward with it.

On my first day of the ballet dance club, we were asked to introduce ourselves. The girl who was sitting next to me introduced herself and added that she has been dancing ballet for over sixteen years. The next girl said she had ten years of experience, and the other one said that they had eleven years of experience. I wondered if I should proceed with even introducing myself or if I should secretly walk away before

I embarrass myself. But the thought came too late. It was my turn. I was the only black person there, so everyone was looking straight at me. I slowly introduced myself and left out of the experience part. As we started stretching, all ready to dance, I hurt myself so bad trying to split my legs. That's when I learned that that club was another mistake. Apparently, American kids start engaging in extracurricular activities that they are interested in at a very young age.

It helped them to discover and work on their talents. I couldn't relate to that because back home, you are only encouraged to engage in school activities such as study groups, homework, and any school material related activities. Other than that, house chores are your extracurricular activities. And if you watch the timeline of my childhood, it was more of a Tarzan-like life.

All these thoughts reminded me my younger brother was very good at soccer. He loved it so much, but my mom couldn't let him go to the soccer practice because she thought that it was an excuse to hangout out with bad kids. Plus, my mom always said that soccer is the reason he doesn't do well in class. That was exactly the reason he disrespected my mom by not doing some of the house chores. This is how talent is suppressed back in my homeland. As the days passed by, I started feeling lost more often. I started missing home and my friends that I had left back at home. I was in a completely different world, and no one was able to understand me. No one could step in my shoes. My back home friends and family thought I was living in paradise and that I have made it in life. I could imagine myself being the exemplar in my family, where everyone held me as the role model.

And me, I couldn't spoil their expectations. There was no way I was going to explain to them that I was struggling to fit in and adjust. They would have immediately thought that I'm being very ungrateful, so I never discussed how I felt with anyone other than my best friend Giella, who was also in the USA.

We would meet and talk and she understood me. Soon, we both became like a therapist to each other. With my other friends and family, all I had as my medium of contact was my phone. So I would mostly be on my phone, texting my family and friends. Eventually, things started changing, and I got very busy with school and work. My friends and family would text me at night when I'd be asleep, and I would reply to them in the morning after eight hours of receiving their text. It ended up affecting our friendship in ways that I was not able to explain to myself. I could just feel the distance between us growing every day, and I could do nothing about it. As a result, I was crying myself to sleep every night missing home, missing the environment, and the love I felt back home.

My life now constituted only of school and work. I had no friends to talk to other than my superficial friends whom we only meet during class lectures. I felt more lonely than I had ever felt in my entire life. I would sometimes spend two whole days without speaking to anyone, just going to class and back to my room to doing homework.

Moreover, it was getting colder and colder every day. I didn't want to be outside, taking even my regular walks, so I stayed indoors for the most part. Some of my friends back home started texting me that I have become too arrogant and too comfortable, saying that's why I don't text back like I used to. I tried to explain to them the time difference and how busy I was. However, they didn't seem to understand. I kept trying to hold on to some of those friendships, fearing to be left utterly alone with no friends, neither back home and nor in the USA. It soon felt like a compulsion to me, trying to force my friendships to work. I did not want to let go, but it was the only option I was left with. Trying to stay up late to talk to my friends back home was messing with my school performance since I was always exhausted in the morning, texting during classes all the time because of the pressure of replying to messages on time.

I had to compromise one of the options since I ultimately was failing to find a balance. It was hurting so bad to lose friends and being blamed for the failed relationship. I had to let them ago anyways and move on. As I let go of trying to force my relationships back home to work, I adopted a new hobby. That was of working out in the gym. I squeezed in the third activity between my work and study.

I would spend several hours at the gym, determined to keep my weight the same regardless of any change in my diet. Most people tend to gain so much weight when they come to the USA, and I was not about to follow the trend. Just like that, I fell in love with exercising, and this hobby happened to fill the gap of lost friendships and overwhelming nostalgia of home. It kept me busier so that I didn't have time to think about whatever was going wrong in my life. It became a perfect escape. I also started involving myself in research about nutrition, eating healthier, and getting used to raw salads. I made peace with myself and with the fact that I was alone. I stopped trying to engage in clubs that I didn't like for the sake of making friends. I also stopped forcing myself to socialize. If it had to happen, if it had to work out, it would work out, I told myself.

With this newfound recovery, life came more naturally to me. As it had happened in my previous school too that when I least tried it was when I made friends, here too similarly, I ended up making two friends in my first semester. With the arrival of Winters, one of my wishes was looking to come true. And that was of experiencing the snowy days, and I was excited. I had been waiting my whole life for that moment, and it was one of the reasons why I chose Michigan State University over Arizona State University.

At the beginning of November, the weather forecast showed it would snow in two days. The office of international students sent us several emails of tips as a guide to survive snowy days. Friends had told me that it gets very slippery during the winters. They said I needed to buy appropriate boots, thermals, beanie, lip balm, and so on. I had too much information in my head about snow, and I wanted lesser of the stress attached to it and more of the experience. The day finally came. Early morning, I saw some white fluffy and soft small ball-like stuff falling from the sky. It looked like popcorn but appeared to be very soft. I went outside to try touching the snow. I was fully dressed up, but I had forgotten to put on gloves. I was walking and admiring the snow and oddly didn't feel too cold. That was until ten minutes passed, and I felt my ears and my fingers start to freeze. I couldn't feel myself.

Following the season, the freezing days began. During the days, I could see the sun outside but would not be able to feel it. Falling multiple times on the slippery snow, trying to catch the bus at the bus stop became a habit. Wearing multiple layers of clothes that made me feel very uncomfortable every day became a routine. Given all of that, my seasonal depression took root in me. The winter blues as they call it. I started having this internal sadness and loneliness. Not being able to see people walk outside because it was too cold made it worse. The school eventually closed for the winter break, and I spent nearly five days talking to no one since everybody had left for Christmas break. I seemed to be the only one who was left in the dorm on my floor. It hit me so hard, spending holidays alone in the coldest environment where you are compelled to stay all the time indoors. Like a snowflake, all my excitement for the snow and the winters just melted like that. During the day, I would try to sit next to the window to feel the sun's reflection and listening to music all day long. I ordered a small speaker from amazon to play Christmas songs that we used to play at home on a loudspeaker. As lonely as it sounds, that was my way to celebrate Christmas.

I know how it sounds, my life was not perfect, but I was still happy to be able to help my family financially. The little happiness that I could feel, I was not going to deny myself that. It was so fulfilling to put a smile on my mom's face whenever I would randomly buy her something. I had made it my goal to send her as many gifts as I could for special events and to celebrate her birthdays since my college job.

She never had any year where she celebrated her birthday throughout her whole married life. I was determined to make the next birthdays and mother's day very special for her. Furthermore, I was also saving to buy my family land to build a house on too. My father died before he was able to build a house for my family, and I had made it my responsibility to finish what he was not able to do. Additionally, I was motivated by the nomadic life I spent my first half of life. We didn't have our own house so we had kept moving around. We shifted nearly every few years, sometimes because the landlord had increased the rent, or he wanted his house back for other businesses.

Other times, we moved because we found a better option. Point being, it was never a stable life. That was probably one of the reasons I never had any place to call home and struggled with belonging. After spending two years at Michigan State University, it was time to go back home for the summer holidays. I started counting the remaining days five months before, and it almost felt like a dream going back to Rwanda.

I planned everything that I was going to do at home. My plans included buying the land for my family, and I had saved the money for that. I was over the moon at the thought of seeing them again and sharing everything about all the little things I hadn't shared ever since I took the flight from Kigali International airport. I had planned to take my mom out for nice dinners as many times as I can and to take her for shopping. I also made a list of everyone close to me and the gifts that I will buy for them. This is how the list went like: shoes and clothes for my brothers; iPhone for my sister; handbags, clothes, perfumes, necklaces, and shoes for my mom: chocolates for everyone; dresses for my aunties and bottles of wine for my uncles and stepdad.

Shopping for everyone at home was very exciting. It felt so good to be able to afford things for everyone that would make them feel delighted. I just couldn't wait to hand it over to them and watch their reactions. My mom is my mom, and she had asked me three months before about what I wanted her to cook for me. She had bought a young male chicken six months before I had gotten there.

She was going to raise it herself and prepare it for me when I got home. She was as excited as I was about the whole prospect. The only thing that was not exciting was the seventeen hours of the flight back home. It was a terrible thought, but I distracted myself from focusing on it. I was just too excited to see my family again. Sometimes I would just sit in class and feel this grin climb on my face out of nowhere at the thought of being home soon. My professors would catch me laughing several times and ask me the reason for it. I told him straight up that I was feeling thrilled in my heart, which was true. The day finally came when I was to fly back home. When I was inside the plane, the flight seemed to be taking forever. I was impatiently waiting to land at Kigali International airport. I was supposed to arrive at 7:30 PM sharp, and my family was aware of that. They all planned to come to the airport to wait for me, and I was invigorated at the thought.

When the flight attendant announced that we should prepare for landing, I brought my head close to the window and took in the views. I started seeing lights and the typical domestic feel that screamed I was in Kigali. My home, where my heart belonged, ah. Tears of joy started streaming from my eyes. I couldn't help myself. My heart was elated and overwhelmed, and I just couldn't stop crying. And this was only upon arrival. I hadn't even met my family yet.

After landing, I went to pick my two big suitcases and proceeded toward the exit door right where I was supposed to meet my family. As I pulled my bags behind me, I kept scanning past the crowd of people who were huddled outside, waiting for their loved ones. I couldn't find my family among them. Here and there, I kept searching but to no avail. I eventually exited the airport and went to where the taxi cars were parked. I was still searching for my family, and in the midst of it, I saw this girl standing by. I asked if I could borrow her phone to call my family as my phone had not been working due to the foreign sim in it. I quickly called my sister, and she said they were running late and will be there in a few minutes.

I had been so worried and frustrated that no one came to pick me up that I had forgotten entirely about the *"African time"* and how laid back people are at home. I was getting mad with every minute I waited for them. I just wasn't expecting them to be late, at least not on a day that meant so much to me.

They finally showed up when I had lost half of the excitement. But it was still heartwarming to see everyone. My mom had stayed home cooking, so she didn't come to the airport. She was the only one who stayed home, and she was calling every minute to make sure I landed safely. When I reached home, I saw they had cooked all sorts of food as if it was a wedding. They had bought an enormous cake that had written on it 'Welcome back Josine.'

Along with that, they had bottles of champagne too, and the whole home and family feel. I had never felt so loved as I felt on that day. We drank, we ate, and we danced, all inside our little home. I will never be able to forget that day and the joy that I had felt. I handed them all the gifts that I had brought for everyone, and we all cheered up as everyone opened their gifts.

All of them loved their presents, but my mom's gifts were the best of all. I primarily had devoted the most time to those. They were carefully selected, and every detail about them was just what she loved. She picked on each one and hugged me tightly. My mom tried on this gorgeous gown dress that I had brought for her, and it fitted her so well. It was so satisfying to watch everyone laugh and excited as they opened their gifts.

The curiosity was making their eyes gleam, and I tell you, doing that to your family is one of the best feelings in the world. That is what I lived for, and I couldn't be more proud of myself. My sister, as usual, rummaged through my clothes and picked everything she liked. And I, of course, let her take them, completely sober this time. I was feeling happy and generous at that moment. Otherwise, we would have fought about it, perhaps. The next morning I went to the beauty salon to get my hair and nails done. It was one of those little things I missed about home. When I got there, my sister guided the stylist on how they should do my nails. When it came to styling, my sister always wanted everything to be perfect. After the styling, I had planned to live in the guest house I had rented.

I arranged a separate house for I was planning to stay out late sometimes. If I was going to stay at home, I would have to abide by my mother's rules of not staying out late. Surprisingly, no one amongst my family asked me about my life in the USA except for my mom. I thought my friends would be asking me all about the USA, but it was surprising to me that they didn't. My mom was the only one who was interested to hear all about it.

She told me that she couldn't sleep that day when I flew to the USA until she heard that I had landed safely. My mother wanted to listen to every detail of my journey to the US, as well as how I managed to survive. She would ask me how many black students were in my class, ask me about food, my dorm, and my roommates. And I more than opened my heart out to her.

On the other hand, the only thing that my friends wanted from me was for me to take them out. They thought I was rich, and they were not the only ones. Everybody from abroad is considered rich in a third-world country. I only wished they would actually ask me how I got the money. I wish they could respect my struggle and understand that going abroad alone did not guarantee a golden future.

I wish they could hear me say that working a job while being a full-time student who is required to maintain her GPA above 3.5 is a tough job. I wanted them to ask me how much I missed home and how I spent countless days alone without speaking to anyone. I wanted them to understand how hard it had been making new friends and losing the old ones.

I also wanted them to ask me about my classes and how I was usually the only black student in a classroom of two hundred. I wanted them to talk about how I struggled to fit in. I also wanted them to ask me about places that I had traveled to, such as New York, California, and Washington DC. But, they never asked any of the above, and all we did was going out with me paying the bills while they take pictures of the food and posting them on social media.

They introduced me to all the new fancy places to hang out at, and they wanted me to buy them pizza and burgers. Our conversation revolved around nothing more than talking about Instagram models and everyone else who was trending at that time. They knew every celebrity and where they hung out at. They followed all the Twitter gossip and Instagram news. For me, every day was a new realization of how much I have outgrown my friends and how different we have become. There was a sense of superficiality I found in them, and yet again, I struggled to fit in. It was just too exhausting.

Luckily, time with friends did not constitute all of my time back home. I had a local internship that kept me busy, and everyone there wanted to know everything about my life in the USA. They asked questions like how did I make it to the USA. How much I get paid at my job, where did I live, how much stipend do I receive. They also asked if I had a white boyfriend?

At certain places, I felt attacked, because most of these questions were personal. I wanted to share about my journey to America but not so openly. I had also forgotten that there is nothing like mind your business back at home. Everyone knows everybody and everything about them. Privacy is an alien concept for most of them. Being in the States had taught me how to respect people's privacy, and I had already adopted the culture. I experienced reverse culture shock every single day, and I suddenly felt like I don't fit at home either. The question now was where did I fit in? Neither in the USA nor at home. Perhaps I should not have been so hard on everyone, but I felt what I felt.

Not a single day passed by without someone asking me to get them, sponsors, when I return back to the USA. Mothers introduced me to their children in school, asking me to find them USA scholarships and schools. Friends asked me to find them white boyfriends/girlfriends, and I was there wondering how easy they think it is to make a friend in the USA, let alone getting a boyfriend or pulling strings for admissions and scholarships.

Questions like bring me an iPhone the next time you come back, or send it to me when you go back to the USA were also getting on my nerves. What was more infuriating was that they weren't implying that they will give me money. Instead, they expected I would have no issues gifting it to them. They thought I was rich and that iPhones are very cheap in the USA. In their minds, they felt they were not asking for much. Given these events, I slowly came to realize that I'm more like a money object to most people back home. They no longer saw me as a friend or cousin but as an ATM or a resource. My brothers, at one point, made it worse when I heard them jokingly calling me 'BNR= National Bank of Rwanda.' It is the main national bank of Rwanda and considered to be very fancy. They called my older sister 'Umwarimu Sacco,' which is the cheapest saving and credit cooperative for Rwandan teachers.

As hard as I tried to blend in, I just couldn't. I had to accept the fact that I neither fit at home nor fit in the USA. And then also accept that it was absolutely okay not to. I decided to pick whatever works for me in both cultures and go with the flow. It was also clear that home is what I would make it be. Home could also be more than a place. It could be, but a feeling and I needed to meditate and find an environment that gave me that feeling.

As my summer kept rolling, I focused on the small goals that I wanted to achieve, such as spending time with my mom and buying the land for my family. I hired a commissioner to help me out, and I spent weeks visiting different areas in different locations until I finally found a place that was good enough for my budget. Everyone approved of it, and we bought the site. I wanted it to be in my mom's name, and that's exactly what I did. The next steps were for me to save enough money again to start building a house on that land. That was something I made it my next three years' goal to be. Apart from buying my family the property, I had also thought about starting a small business that would generate income for my family instead of me sending them money monthly.

I figured that if I genuinely wanted to save money to build them a house, then I needed to find a way to stop sending money regularly. My sister and I discussed it at length, and we took a small loan to add to the five thousand dollars I had remaining with me. We then bought a share in my uncles' company, and that provided a substantial amount of money to pay for my brothers' tuition fees, my sister's needs, and my family's house rent bills.

My sister and I were the only ones who knew about the business, and we agreed to keep it a secret. That way, my family would still think that I send them money directly from the USA – where I was soon to return. Otherwise, they would have asked me for more. Anytime there was a need for cash at home, I would tell my sister to send home whatever they needed, and this worked out wonderfully. It helped me to start saving up for a house as well. Nevertheless, I was also thinking about my plans after graduation, and I had to save enough money to buy a car and to survive, or instead thrive after graduation before I acquired a job.

My life seemed to be infused with purpose, and I was feeling euphoric towards what I had achieved within a span of two years. But as it happens in life, I was also terrified of what was to come after graduation. The business soon started going well. Alongside that, there was one more thing I wanted to do for my family before the year ended, which was helping my family move from the town they lived in into another town. This would help my mom change jobs.

My mom had complained multiple times about the neighborhood that we lived in. She hated it, and she always wished she lived somewhere else. The feeling was mutual to be honest, for I also hated the community ever since I had got poisoned with that stomach thing. I had this quaint hatred towards that place, and I couldn't wait to move away from there. I also did not like the fact that my mom was still working from 7 AM to 5 PM as a teacher who got paid less than $70 a month. It wasn't worth it at all. My sister and I discussed moving our family, and as soon as we told them about the idea, they were up for it. My mom started calling rental agencies right away to help us find a place to rent in a new town that she wanted to move into. My mom also sent out a resignation letter the same week. It was a sigh of relief, for she too had been extremely fed up with her job and that neighborhood.

One week later, a rental house had been arranged, and they were ready to move out. It happened so quickly that I realized how much everyone has been waiting for this moment. My family finally moved almost one hundred miles away from where they used to live. The new town was beautiful, and the new apartment was a significant upgrade from where we had been living.

They had nothing but good things to say about it. I cherished the fact that they didn't have to worry about the rental cost since my business took care of that. Hearing about their delight, I wished I was at home to celebrate with them. But I commemorated it in my own way, privately. I bought a sparkling wine to celebrate alone in my dorm, countries away. I won't lie, though, I could still feel the joy and celebration in my tiny space that was going on back home. That was the year of 2017 for me, and my God, it was indeed a blessing. To both my family and me. It was the spiking point when I experienced my dreams coming true. I had so many reasons to be thankful and proud.

And so, after fifteen years of being a teacher, my mom dropped that work and started a small business of selling African prints. All she had needed was $500, which I had given her. She had no pressure to make a living from it since the business was taking care of the big bills such as rental, school fees, and gas. We all bought African prints to support my mom's new business and obviously bought two for her as well.

I had spent so much of my time focusing on my family that I the realization dawned upon me: I don't have a life for myself. My sole source of happiness had become my family, and I figured I hadn't focused on myself in a very long while. I literally had nothing special going in my life, no leisure, not even having fun because of spending all my savings on my family and friends. I had been sacrificing my pleasure for my family's, and I had been happy with it because, since childhood, I had made it my life purpose. To be honest, it was quite fulfilling. I knew that my life is not only for myself but also for those who rely on me for living and expenses. Despite the positivity of this, the thought would scare me every day. I had to be successful by all means; there was no alternative in my life. But you know, the fear of failing has kept me from dating since I was petrified of getting pregnant. I mean, I knew how to prevent it, but I also knew of the risks. I was just not willing to take them.

I had to always lay it down before any guy who tried to approach me that I'm not ready for sex. I told them if that's a deal-breaker, then we can't be together. That being said, I must confess I remained single. It was hard to find a guy who would commit to a sex-free dating.

I was afraid of pregnant to the extent that I always had condoms in my bad, regardless of my being sexually inactive and whether I had a boyfriend or not. I told myself that I would be ready after graduation once I have my degree and my full-time job. I knew that that way if anything happened, I would still survive. Besides, I was not going to date anyone who was penniless. My preferences were wealthy and successful older men who had made something of their lives.

So even my dating preferences were well-thought-of. I was confident that men older than me would be responsible if my worst nightmare of getting pregnant happened. You can expect older dudes to be more experienced and them having gone through relatively more practical struggles to reach a good place in their lives. Plus, I also had dad issues, so I always tried to find a dad figure in men among those I would seek to date.

Don't get me wrong; I am no elitist or classicist. I have nothing against the destitute and will not shy away from helping them when I can afford to. It's only that dating an impoverished person for me was more like having one more person that I had to take care of in my life. I was not supportive of that. I had to think about myself. I probably wanted someone to take care of me now, yes financially too, but more like in a well-rounded way.

As I got closer to my last college year, I started putting together all the possible plans of life post-graduation. I had the goal of having at least ten grand saved up to help me with moving out, re-locating, and paying monthly bills before I get a job. I also wanted to get a driver's license and purchase a car right after graduation to help me with the moving out process. My plan A was to get an OPT (Optional Practical Training) job, which was a work permit available for international students. Since I was a science major, I was allowed to work for three years in the USA without an employer sponsoring me. My plan B was to apply for a graduate school, and my worst-case scenario was to be deported if nothing else worked out, which also meant that I needed to have a plan of what I will do if I find myself back home.

Life did not get any easier with designing the above plans. I worked tirelessly to save money, studied to have an excellent GPA for graduate school application, and spent hours studying for GRE. I never desired to go to graduate school right after my undergraduate education. My foremost plan was to get a great job and have an employer sponsoring my MBA that I had planned to study online.

Managing to do all of the above simultaneously had me going through exhilarating, stressful sessions, and having a constant headache. I was so burned out that I once and a while, subconsciously entered men's room. I was always running to save time, and I almost lost control of myself. Managing stress has never been easy for me, and taking a step back was not an option since I was very much scared to go with one plan. I had to keep on keeping on. To feel relief and take care of myself better, I started researching ways to manage stress. Ultimately, I came up with a meditation plan that I followed before my sleep time. Investing in yoga sessions also became a de-stressing activity.

The only problem was that I hardly had free time. In the midst of that, doing everything at once led to GRE failure, and I was not about to invest more money into retaking the test. Instead, I devised another plan, which was applying for a graduate school in Canada that didn't require the GRE prerequisite.

It turned out that graduate school applications are also time-consuming occupations, especially when you are applying to full scholarships. So I was looking at writing five essays for only one graduate school. Deep down, I knew that the right thing to do was to give up the graduate school application option since it was not even what I wanted. But on the conflicting side, I was too scared to give that up as well, for what if I ended up in limbo? I eventually decided to apply to one school instead. I never expected to get in, but I wanted to have tried it just in case.

One day, given all the stress of hectic activities, I was running toward the bus station. One of my friends looked at me and advised me to seek help because the pressure was too much. She gave me the contact number for the counseling center at Michigan State University, but I knew that if try to see a therapist, they will advise me to narrow down my plans and stick to one.

We all can expect that was something I would not want to hear. But I also knew that my health should come first no matter what. So I had to squeeze a middle way out. Instead of a therapist, I started having these long calls with my best friend, Giella, who seemed to understand my struggles. She was the only person who understood my life and my hustles. Plus, she is brilliant and knowledgeable with a mature sense of reasoning.

She might not know that she helped me during that phase, and amidst that phase, but she did become my therapist. She was the only one I could be vulnerable with. Being an international student in the USA also meant that getting a job was ten times harder than for domestic students. Most companies were not willing to hire international students due to the increased cost of sponsoring them. You had to be extremely smart and ten times better than a native to get a job. Even though OPT allowed us to work with no required sponsorship, employers were not willing to invest in someone who will require sponsorship in one or three years to come. On top of that, most employers had limited knowledge about OPT, and they hated the paperwork that came with hiring international students.

After learning about this stress, I started applying for jobs eight months before graduation. It was unfortunate that all I was getting were rejection letters. I had made it my goal to send at least five job applications per day. With the many applications I submitted, I also received many rejections along with it. I had never experienced that much rejection in my life, and it was depressing.

With that contaminated mind, I started questioning my self-worth and whether I was actually good enough for the jobs that I was applying to. I had my resume checked multiple times with Career Services at the university, and I even tried to compare my resume to my friends'. I couldn't find any real factor that explained the number of rejections I was receiving. Four months into the job hunting with no luck, I started losing all hopes I previously had about getting a job. At that point, it had gotten too late to apply for another graduate school. The following week, I got a rejection letter from also the one grad school I had applied to. For the first time in my life, I didn't seem to have control over my life despite trying everything in my power. Can you picture it? A girl like me who always had several plans and contingency options, who still had one of those options work out, nothing was working out for her. She was in an abyss. I couldn't get what was coming next after graduation for me.

The only plan that I had remaining was to keep on applying for jobs and hope. I now set another goal of sending at least ten applications a day. I applied to anything and everything available in my field of study. I wished I was allowed to apply to jobs outside my field of study, but as an international student, that was not an option.

The pressure of getting a job increased when I learned that after you have applied for OPT employment authorization, you are given a three month grace period to find a job before getting deported. So, I had three months after graduation time to get a job or get deported. And that became my brand new nightmare.

The only thing that kept me going at that point was that I was not alone. Almost every international student was in the boat as me. We would sometimes joke about it and make folders for rejection letters. As desperate as I was, I heard about this nutritional training that you have to pay $3000 for, and they guarantee you a full-time job as a dietary technician after successful training. I ended up applying for it, and I had planned that if I didn't get a job a month after graduation, I would definitely go with the training since it was within my field of study.

As my graduation day approached, I decided that I was going to have a fun and joyous graduation regardless of my situation. I braced myself for the truth that no one from amongst my family members was going to attend my graduation since it was too expensive to travel to the USA. I comforted myself with the belief that my graduation day will be what I will make it. I can either decide to do absolutely nothing or try to have as much fun as I can afford to. I decided to celebrate myself by buying at least three dresses for my graduation and having a professional photoshoot. I had a few college friends around who were willing to party with me on the night of my graduation.

Two days before my graduation day, I gave myself a break from job hunting and focused all my energy on what I have achieved throughout my college years. I reflected on my journey and felt very grateful for everything I was able to do. I admired how much I had developed and all the bad things I had outgrown. I took time to thank myself for making my dreams come true and bringing me where I was, and for being strong enough to handle whatever life threw on me. When I stepped on the graduation stage to receive my degree, inside my chest, I carried a grateful heart. After that, I partied the whole night. I had the most extraordinary graduation, and I enjoyed every moment of it.

Eventually, that milestone passed. My life did not get any easier the day after graduation. I had to find an apartment right away and prepare for moving out of the dorm. I had no clue where I should or was going to be moving to since I did not have a job yet. I had researched the cheapest cities to move to in the United States, but again moving without a set purpose did not seem like a great plan. I was left with only one option of pursuing nutritional training. You can imagine that thinking about paying three thousand dollars at that point hurt, but it seemed to be the only thing that was right to do. The training was based in Columbus, Ohio, which was at a four hours drive from Michigan State University. Since I had decided to go ahead with the training, I also entertained the idea of moving to Columbus, especially given it was among the cities I had researched about, too, where I had been potentially planning to move to. The training started soon, even before I got an apartment. I was called in for it only three days a week. Several hectic bus rides from Michigan to Columbus later, and after renting a private room to stay in for three days, I was set.

The first private room I booked had strict rules of checking in before 11 PM. According to the bus schedule, I was supposed to be there by 5 PM. There was no straight bus that went to Columbus, so I had to go through multiple bus shifts, which made it a ten hours trip instead of four.

When I got to my first bus stop around 7 PM, where I was supposed to have a switch, I found out that my bus will be delayed for three hours, which eventually became four. So I ended up spending four hours at the bus stop that night. It was so cold and rainy, all I could think about was how did I go from a fun graduation night to spending a sleepless night at the bus stop? Life was changing on me very quickly.

Following a cherishable 2017, I was stuck in an arduous 2019. My bus showed four hours later, and I arrived at Columbus around 3 AM, which was way past my checking-in time. So I spent another night at the bus stop, completely lost in a new city. I thought about spending time in some coffee shop, but all the cafes around were closed. I didn't want to go too far in an unknown city at 3 AM in the morning. Who knew what awaited in the dark.

My training was supposed to start at 8 AM. As soon it was 7 AM, I retried to find a coffee shop and succeeded. I quickly had some breakfast before taking an Uber to my training. There was nothing too impressive about the training. It was just a tedious and awful day.

After the third day of my training, I went straight to the bus stop to wait for my bus that was scheduled to depart at 9 PM to Michigan. When I got there, for some reason, the bus was again delayed by two hours. I sat at the bus stop for three hours until I was informed that the bus to Michigan was canceled. It was almost 1 AM in the morning, and it was too late to book a room to sleep in. I googled to find a nearby library that would open and found it. I took a twenty minutes Uber ride to reach the library and pretended to read books as

I spent my night there. Libraries are safe, and they had WiFi that allowed me to watch a movie all night long. So it was my own little hack. Early in the morning, I had no means of getting back home except waiting for another evening bus. And who knew if that bus might get canceled or delayed too. I was fed up with buses, and basically everything in general. I couldn't imagine retaking a bus, so I decided to google a car dealership so that I could finally buy a car.

I had planned to buy a car after graduation anyway. It was just that I hadn't felt like it was the right time. On the flip side, I had also learned that in life, you just can't always wait for the right time, definitely not for everything. Sometimes you have to give up on waiting and start doing. I had been spending so much money taking Ubers and buses, plus I was jobless, so buying a car felt like the right thing to do at the moment. For all we knew, perhaps that was the sign that it was the right time.

Now, I wanted a big car in which I could sleep in if it came to that. I needed it to be big enough to fit all my belongings in. But now here's the thing. I was by no means a motorhead. I did not know cars, and I didn't know what I should be looking for when I get to the dealership. I only knew that I'm looking for a big reliable car that is within my budget. I wished I had someone who would help me, but then again, I was all alone, just like usual. Before I went to the used car dealership, I did a quick research on things that I should look for in a used car. I etched down the list and went ahead to a nearby car dealership. Before I tried to talk to anyone there, I made prayer so that God would help me. The last thing I wanted was to get scammed or taken advantage of since I was already struggling so much. I was drained from two sleepless nights and felt so stuck, but I had no option other than staying stronger.

Once inside, I met this elderly man who had been working at that dealership for about twenty years. I told him the truth of what I was looking for and revealed that I had limited knowledge about cars. He was empathetic towards me, and I could trust him. We connected just like that, and he left everything he was doing to devote himself entirely to helping me find the right car within my budget. He took it upon himself to help me find a great car. He even went ahead and asked the company manager about other cars they had in another location in case there was a better deal available for me. I loved that he was genuinely helpful to me, and I did nothing other than listening to his life stories as he facilitated me. We spent an entire day together, waiting for a car that he said will be a perfect fit for me. It was just that the vehicle was in another location. Finally, after a long wait, the jeep wrangler-like Nissan Xterra cruised in, and I fell in love with it immediately. It was precisely what I was looking for, large enough to fit all my belongings and it reminded me of a jeep wrangler, which happened to be my dream car. I had no complaints.

The older man took my car to the car inspection and had it thoroughly inspected. He also changed the oil, which the car inspector said was old. He made sure the car was good to go. He helped me finalize the whole car insurance, which I had no clue about. He indeed was as if heaven-sent, there to help me out and neutralize the bad taste of past months.

At the end of the day, I was delighted with my purchase, and he seemed happy to meet me too. He asked me to add him on Facebook before we hugged and said our goodbyes. I had been dreaming of the day I would buy my first car and I couldn't believe it had just happened. I drove my car back home that evening, listening to my favorite afrobeat music as I also sing louder than my car speaker. I fell in love with my car, and the love kept increasing with time. I would sometimes merely stare at it and laugh because it was just perfect. By all standards, it was my dream ride. As usual, I celebrated my new car by myself for this achievement by taking myself out to this lovely Chinese restaurant. Giella was the first to know via phone, and she was so thrilled that it was as if the car was hers.

Having a car made my life very easy, especially with the moving out process. I drove back to Michigan, intending to pack all of my belongings and move to Columbus for good. I had also found a temporary apartment to sublease for two months. That was going to buy me more time to find a permanent residence.

Moreover, I also hoped that I would have figured out my life in two months and maybe have a stable job then. I was confident that I had a plan for that moment, and then experience showed me the finger again. I received a call from the nutritional training manager saying that they will not proceed with me because the company that was supposed to employ us after training doesn't hire OPT students. They asked me if I have a green card, I said I don't, and that was it. I explained that my work permit would allow me to work for three years without employer sponsorship. I even made it clear that after three years, I will go to graduate school, so they won't have to sponsor me. The manager said that it was a company rule, and they use so many resources to invest in new employees. They told me they couldn't invest in someone who will leave soon. I didn't know how to react to that terrible news. I just said, *"Okay,"* and was ready to go back to my room and cry oceans.

Just when I had thought I was finally getting my life together, this happened. I was left with questions like should I proceed to move to Columbus, or should I stay? I had told everyone in my friends and family that I had gotten a job in Columbus, and they praised the Lord for me. I finally had an answer to the dreadful questions like, *"What's your plan after graduation."*

You couldn't go a day without someone asking a senior student this question. Someone who hasn't figured their next step hated this question. But of course, those who already had their plans lined up found it very easy to answer. It was even an opportunity for some people to relate their achievement stories. In my case, I had spent months dodging this question because I didn't have an answer to it. I would simply say that I'm still figuring it out, but that was until graduation. After that, I had decided to say that I have a job even though I didn't have any. That became a real hell, especially when the training too was rejected. Since I had already spent so much money going back and forth to Columbus and paying for my apartment deposit, I decided to move to Columbus anyway. There was no better option in my inventory. It was going to save me money and embarrassment from everyone I had already told that I had a job in Columbus.

At the same time, another part of me wanted to go somewhere new, where no one knew me. Life was becoming so hard that I just felt like I wanted to disappear, be forgotten, or be thrown in a completely new environment. Moving to Columbus with absolutely no job or purpose was a risk, but in the end, I settled with that risk. It still made me feel like I was starting afresh. I thought that being in a new place was going to be a distraction to my personal problems. My family had no idea what I was going through, and I intended to keep it just like that. I didn't want them to worry about me. The only person who knew my life details was Giella. She was my go-to person who somehow seemed to understand me on a personal level. Our connection was not one-sided either. We synced so much that we found each other to be in the same situation because she had graduated as well and was struggling. In Columbus, I used google maps for everything, navigating my new city alone and trying to stay alive. It became more like survival, for I was also running low on my savings. The ideal option was I needed to cut down on my expenses by doing things such as eating twice a day instead of three times.

I spent most of my days in my little room that I rented applying for jobs in Columbus. And not to mention, crying as well. To keep my blues from sinking too deep, I tried to walk around as much as I could and jog. It seemed to help since I wasn't going to buy a gym membership. Despite the difficult point in my life, I stuck to staying healthy as much as I could.

I understood that if I got sick, no one was going to help me. So my plan was not to allow myself to get sick. I ate vegetables and fruits every day, and I jogged regularly. Sometimes I would follow some online workout regime, some yoga class, and so on. No matter how hard life got, I always found a way to cope with it healthily. It is the one thing that I can't compromise on, and I love that about myself. Remember my mentors Barbara, Mary, and Michelle? They all contacted me and were worried about me being in a new city alone. It meant a great deal to me that they cared. Even though I wasn't, I tried to convince them that I was fine. There was little they could do anyway, and I wanted to figure out my life on my own.

Since I was on a budget, I could hardly find something fun to do that was also free. I wanted to explore the city and probably go out clubbing and dancing to forget my pains away, but I was financially limited. I came up with a solution to join an online dating site. I figured I would meet guys there who would take me out and pay for me. That way, I would get to explore the cities by also dining out for free.

The plan worked out, and I started going on more than three dates a week. It worked so wondrously! I found myself dining out at almost all the beautiful places in Columbus, and that too all for free. I met bored young men who needed companionship, and we sometimes planned to hike or go to the beach together. I made sure that it didn't get to the point of kissing or doing anything physical.

Sometimes after the first date, I would just cut off with them and avoid a second date. Other times, I would friendzone them, and I adapted and learned techniques to make them not desire for me too much. I ended up having more and more guy-friends, who helped me explore the city. But I wasn't all evil here. I sometimes offered a second date, and during that, I made sure they didn't spend on me. I would suggest going to places like a park or the club, and I would just drink water to avoid the expenditure on both ends.

All in all, I had a lot of fun going on dates with the random guys I met online. I was not scared since I had nothing to lose, and I had become so fearless that nothing seemed to scare me anymore. I was a good judge of character and ensured that I didn't fall for any cheap tricks. I experienced my dream dates and also my worst dates.

But both had a thrill of their own, and I liked it. It was the only exciting thing going on in my life. One month after my graduation, I found myself a part-time job that only gave me ten hours a week to spare. But it was good to be away for those ten hours per week. Now at this point, I was left with two months to find a job, or I was going to get deported. This realization I usually kept at the back of my mind, but over time, it got me worrying more and more. I kept applying to as many jobs as I could. By God's grace, I finally got a promising interview with one company for a quality assurance position. The job was way below my standards, but I was too desperate for one, hence accepted it. I was finally employed full-time, which kept me from getting deported. Honestly speaking, I still felt miserable since it was not even close to an excellent job. But I let it be for the moment and not stress too much.

The employers at the company wanted me to start as soon as possible. Two days after my interview, I showed up for my first day of work. My shift was supposed to begin at 5:30 in the morning, and gratefully, the office was within 30 minutes' drive from my place. I went to work full of hopes, thinking that I have finally made it.

I had no idea the work environment would be temperature controlled. They kept the workspace below 20 F degrees; it was basically freezing all the time. I had to wear water boots to work, a long whitish lab-like coat, two hairnets, goggles, and a beard net. Believe me when I say I couldn't see or feel myself. My body would freeze to the point where I could hardly move, yet I was supposed to stand for ten hours. My back would ache, and I just couldn't believe this was going to be my life. An average shift would seem to take forever for me, and I couldn't wait to leave from there. Finally, when my first day at work came to an end, I was physically sick down to every bone. My whole body was aching. My sister and I have back pain problems that we got from carrying things that weighed more than us when we were young. Hence, when we stand for hours, the back pain surfaces again.

As much as I needed the job, I had to decide and quit after my first day. I couldn't compromise my health for a job. My health came first to me. That job was going to make me feel more miserable than when I didn't have it. I knew it was a hard decision to make considering my situation. I knew that no one would have agreed with me, but deep down, it felt like the right thing to do. I had hoped to find a better option.

After quitting my job, I found another part-time job that was also terrible but not as much as the first one. It was working in a restaurant. I thought I could work part-time as I kept on waiting for a perfect position. On my first day at work, the manager put me in the kitchen to prepare food instead of serving meals. All I had to do was follow the book recipes to prepare some salsa sauces, guacamole, bread toast. I had to wash dishes on the side too. I looked at myself, all tired with food spills all over me, and questioned if this was actually better. I was a brilliant 100% scholarship student, and this was how my future was looking like. The environment at this job was not cold, but the job was strenuous. It required standing the whole time. Two hours at my first shift, I was already ready to quit. My back pain returned, and I felt fatigued. I felt the despondency, but I also told myself that I was being childish. I told myself that I should push through and make this work as I wait for another professional job.

I went for a second shift, and while on my second shift, I accidentally spilled food and oils on the floor. The manager gave me a look that told me that I might not get paid. I washed dishes almost the whole time; this shift gave me a definite confirmation of quitting, which I did immediately after getting off work. One thing about me that I can't deny is that I never settle for anything less, no matter how hard the situation is. And when it came to my health, my standards definitely got higher.

I kept on applying, and after three weeks, I got a call from a random recruiter saying that they saw my resume online, and they have a position to fill. They were looking for someone who had a degree in food science, and I was the perfect candidate. It turned out that the job was a five-month contract job with a company that I had always dreamed of working for. I put the phone down and was ready to celebrate.

I found myself a job that finally allowed me to be in an office environment in a clean fancy looking place. Working with professionals in my industry and being able to wear my professional clothes and my heels as I walked to my office, I felt back on the rails of fulfilling my dream. As always, life looked promising and was finally repay me after all kinds of misery.

I couldn't wait to start my new job. This time I planned to refocus on saving money to build my family a house as soon I accumulated enough money. As my career started, for the first time, I felt like I was at a place where I belonged. My job was perfect, and here I had my own office too. It was everything I had wanted in a job, and I was wrapped up in ecstasy.

After so long, I started feeling great about myself again. I would go to work overdressed every day, looking elegant and extremely professional. I had always envisioned myself as an independent working woman, and there was that Josine that finally emerged in the mirror.

My one-bedroom apartment was also beautiful, located in a respectable neighborhood with a nice pool and a gym in the apartment complex. I was making homemade green smoothies every morning for breakfast, dancing in my room after work, and going out to bars on Saturday night. Of course, the church followed on Sunday mornings.

It was a strange turn of events, and I loved it so much. My life returned to colors and blossoming, and everything reminded me that my purpose was back. I felt like I couldn't be any happier than I was. I finally found a home in every sense: be it in terms of residence, occupation, family satisfaction, or nationality. I tasted what home finally was. It was the feeling of experiencing a wild and tortuous journey through the forest and finally making to a place I had always dreamed about.

NOT THE HOME I DREAMED ABOUT

www.ingramcontent.com/pod-product-compliance
Lightning Source LLC
Chambersburg PA
CBHW022136170626
46807CB00005B/1960